The Chopin Express

BY HOWARD KAPLAN

The Damascus Cover

The

Chopin Express

Howard Kaplan

E.P. DUTTON • NEW YORK

For information contact:
E.P. Dutton, 2 Park Avenue, New York, N.Y. 10016

Library of Congress Cataloging in Publication Data

Kaplan, Howard S.
The Chopin express.

I. Title.
PZ4.K17328Ch   [PS3561.A558]   813'.5'4   78-5567

ISBN: 0-525-08040-6

Published simultaneously in Canada by
Clarke, Irwin & Company Limited, Toronto and Vancouver

Designed by The Etheredges

10 9 8 7 6 5 4 3 2 1

First Edition

For
Michael Blankfort
and
Arthur Hertzberg

September 1

One-Vienna

A chilled wind rushed across the outdoor Ostbahn platform rattling the corrugated iron awnings overhead. The Colonel pushed up the lapels of his woolen jacket and sucked distastefully on an Austrian Smart cigarette. He missed his Dunhill Montecruz cigars, but the dossiers of rival intelligence services detailed that he smoked them; when away from Israel he made do with the indigenous tobacco.

Sleeping on the bench next to the Colonel was a blond-haired, unshaven man with a cane hooked between his legs. He suddenly tossed inside some nightmare, striking the Colonel with his cane. The head of Israeli Intelligence rose and moved away—just as a contingent of twelve uniformed Austrian policemen clutching 9mm Walther MPL submachine guns turned the corner around Track 7.

The anti-terrorist commandos sought the early morning shadows. Fanning out in pairs, they stationed themselves at ten-yard intervals. Two extra teams covered Track 2, where at seven-ten the Chopin Express would slip into Vienna's Südbahnhof station, thirty-one hours after departing Moscow. The Colonel crossed the platform and stood at the edge of Track 1. The icy wind struck his face, pulling the blood to his cheeks. Minutes later two white Volkswagens, topped with rotating blue lights and plates that read POLEZEI, slammed to a halt by Track 7, parking near the Jewish Agency vans that were waiting to rush Russian refugees to the old Red Cross station near Schwechat Airport.

As the train approached a whistle blew. Policemen tightened their forefingers around the triggers of their machine guns. Four officers, wearing white shirts and loosely fitting sport coats, their hair uniformly close-cropped and neatly combed, rode the escalator up from the lower level.

The blue and yellow TU 2 locomotive screeched toward the station. Before the engine stopped two dozen armed Bundes Gendarmerie in gray slacks and gray woolen sweaters bounded off the moving train and trotted out of the station. Policemen, baggage carriers, and Jewish Agency people rushed to the passenger cars. Windows were yanked open and luggage thrust toward waving hands. People, in tears and with dazed expressions, emerged from the train. Security personnel, their machine guns leveled in readiness, tried to sift the Russian Jewish emigrants from the Czech and Polish travelers.

The Colonel glanced at an old man clutching onto the Israeli baggage carrier, tears running down his face, and turned to leave. He wanted to direct his thoughts to his mission but the old refugee's tear-slashed face stuck in his mind. Angrily he walked faster. The Colonel disliked emotional responses, particularly his own. By the time he reached the escalator his thoughts were fully under control.

The blond, unshaven tramp, now seated on the bench, followed him with clear eyes. He was Alexandr Mikhailovich Zavorin, head of the First Chief Directorate of the KGB.

The Colonel crossed Wiedner Gürtel Avenue under a maze of electric tram wires. Fiats, Toyotas, small Mercedes, Opels, and VW's clogged the cobbled intersection at Prinz Eugenstrasse. The Colonel headed for the tram station across from the Belvedere Palace gardens.

He boarded a red D tram, which wobbled up the narrow street. Near the tarnished statue of Karl Von Schwarzenberg, riding on a frothing stallion, the trolley shifted tracks; electricity sizzled overhead. When the motorman stopped at the Schubertring, a section of the broad tree- and grass-bordered boulevard that circles the inner city, the Colonel descended the narrow wood steps to the street. At a nearby kiosk he ordered a wurst, served with a squirt of mustard and a slice of rye bread, on a plate covered with a sheet of waxed paper. Leaning against the wooden stall, he ate slowly, without appetite. His eyes swept the street and sidewalk, focusing on people similarly at rest. He dumped the half-eaten sausage in a trashcan and walked away, then as if changing his mind, he turned back toward the kiosk, eyes darting. He asked for a Schwechater lager, declined a glass, and brought the bottle to his lips. Seeing nothing suspicious, he bought an extra slice of bread, slipped it into his pocket, and headed for the Stadtpark.

The sun rising above the Hilton Hotel at the northeast corner of the park began to warm the fall morning. The Colonel tossed bits of bread into the mossy water of an artificial pond edged with oaks and weeping willows. Ducks glided toward him and snatched the food, the splash of their bills creating concentric ripples that widened toward the shore.

"Lovely day," a man said from behind the Colonel. His German carried an unmistakable American accent.

Though he'd seen and heard him approach, the Colonel didn't turn.

"It's a pleasant surprise to see you in Vienna," the man continued.

The Colonel tossed his last bit of bread into the green water. Three ducks noisily converged on the spot where it landed.

The man spoke again. "It's well known that you rarely leave Israel and . . ."

"Why don't we walk," the Colonel said, irritated that this CIA agent had mentioned his country of origin while they were stationary. In that position the likelihood of their conversation being monitored was greatly increased.

They moved off along a paved path, both men silent. Phillip Fleske, a Psychological Warfare and Paramilitary staff officer working for the Clandestine Services division of the CIA, was currently liaison with British Military Intelligence, MI-5, in London. Fleske, past fifty, stocky and pale from years in England, wore a beige jeans suit. His hair was clipped short. Silver-white a few years ago, it now seemed a lifeless gray. His brown-tinted

6

sunglasses hid small eyes, perpetually red from long hours of work and relentless insomnia.

The Colonel took Fleske's sleeve and, moving off the walkway onto the damp grass, guided him in a hundred-and-eighty-degree turn. A movie camera with a telephoto lens might otherwise have photographed their conversation which could later be deciphered by specially trained lip readers.

"The message you are to carry to our friends in London is crucial," the Colonel began in a low monotone. "You must convince them that the Soviet agent we apprehended committed suicide before he could talk. I assume you've been briefed."

"Yes, quite thoroughly. My people asked me to give the matter top priority. I'm on the ten-forty flight to England." A dark bird burst out of a tree to their left, temporarily diverting the American's attention. "One thing I don't understand," he continued as they turned again. "You already sent a courier with instructions. Why did you come yourself?"

"We've had a lot of problems with the transit station here, KGB agents coming through posing as Jews. It requires my attention."

Fleske, aware that the Colonel was rarely so candid, became uneasy. "We share your concern. Presently almost half of those coming out of Russia are settling in Europe, the U.S., and Canada. The potential threat to American security is ominous."

"And to my country's. At the moment we are attempting to discover the methods the Soviets are using to communicate with their operatives. Apprehension of agents will follow as a matter of course." The Colonel paused. "Our primary objective must be to locate the Soviet sleeper agents."

"Washington is willing to cooperate," Fleske said. He was going to say anxious to cooperate, but he decided not to. "My superiors were very pleased your people uncovered their microdot transmission network. That system of theirs is absolutely ingenious. How did you get onto it?"

"You see," the Colonel said, pushing a leaf with his foot, "the important thing is to keep the Soviets ignorant of how much we've learned." An acidy sensation that had been building for some time in the Colonel's stomach suddenly passed into uncomfortable burning. He reached into his pocket for a tablet, finding instead a scrap of chalky cellophane wrapping. He'd chewed his last antacid early that morning. "They mustn't find out we're onto them," the Colonel repeated, frustrated about the tablet.

"Agreed. But I've been instructed to tell you, sir, that the Deputy Director of Plans has ordered The Company to give penetration of the new Soviet offensive missile system priority. Of course," he continued quickly, "the search for sleeper agents will remain one of our secondary objectives." He moved away from the Israeli. "MI-5, I might add, agrees with the DDP."

Those fools, the Colonel thought to himself. If I had their money and resources. . . . He forced a nod. "I understand your position. Tell the DDP to contact me if I can be of assistance. We should work together whenever possible." Anticipating that he'd be left to go it alone again, the Colonel had already plotted his course of action.

"I'll do that. I'm sure he'll be pleased to hear you've offered to help."

Slowly the Colonel withdrew a crumpled pack of cigarettes from his jacket pocket. He took one, then extended the pack to Fleske, who had trouble getting a cigarette out. Finally wedging two stubby fingers into the hole, tearing the paper, he managed to extract one. The Colonel lit his and the hot air entered his lungs. He exhaled quickly and threw the cigarette to the ground. A few years before, anxious for respite from the laborious theorizing of his administrative position, he had relished his occasional journeys to the field. Now he detested leaving Israel; from the first day out he longed for the control over his life he could maintain in his office. He wanted a cigar instead of these biting cigarettes.

Fleske coughed, and began to wheeze uncontrollably. The Colonel stopped walking and waited. A long minute passed before the American could compose himself. "Sorry," he said. "I'm outdoors most of the time . . . the damp weather, it seems to have gotten to me."

"You ought to have yourself checked out."

Fleske nodded. "I've been meaning to."

They started walking toward the cement-lined tributary of the Donau Canal that sliced through the eastern length of the park. "You realize," the Colonel said, "the Russians have increased their infiltration of young agents into the West. It seems they intend to let these kids *sleep* for decades if necessary before activating them. They could do a tremendous amount of damage, left unchecked."

Fleske bit on the edge of the cigarette trying, unsuccessfully, to suppress a cough. "Speaking about kids," he said in a strained voice, "what are we going to do about Steve Barth?"

The Colonel looked at Fleske, the wrinkles around his eyes tightening. "The boy's been on my mind a lot," he said, pleased, for he had been guiding the conversation toward this subject.

"His memory is beginning to return."

"So I've been told."

"It's most unfortunate. I'd hoped he wouldn't become a problem."

"Hope is of little value," the Colonel said. "The boy knows too much."

"That's your fault," Fleske countered.

"Yes, I'm afraid it is. But the matter couldn't be helped."

"You never should have let him find out about the microdots!"

"You're absolutely right, but discussing what should have happened will not solve our present predicament." The Colonel pushed his hands in his pockets. "Where is the boy now?"

"At Claybury Hospital in Woodford Green, just outside London."

"And the extent of what he remembers?"

"Minimal, but it's growing daily. He's been asking about Susan. He wants to know what happened to her."

"Has he been told?"

"No. The doctors think if they do tell him, everything might snap into place." Fleske paused, forming clearly in his mind the conclusion the Colonel had already reached. "It appears he will remember everything soon."

"I see. What do you suggest we do?"

Fleske looked off into the gray sky. A line of bright light shone above the horizon. "There is really no alternative if we are to protect our advantage over the Russians."

"I suppose so," the Colonel said. "What kind of security arrangements are there at the hospital?"

"Minimal. There's rarely a guard at the gate . . . and the man stationed outside his room, he's ours of course."

"I thought he might be."

"I'll use potassium. It's untraceable and relatively painless."
"Yes, good idea. We should spare the boy further pain." The
Colonel stopped and stared down at the muddy stream, trickling
north toward the Donau Canal.

Fleske coughed in the silence, then glanced at his watch. "If
I'm to make the ten-forty flight I should be going."

"Yes, yes. I understand." The Colonel clasped Fleske's hand.
It felt warm and damp. "Good luck," he said. Then he moved off
into the trees.

Across the canal, parked on Am Heumarkt Street parallel to
the white plaster statue of Johann Strauss the Younger, KGB
Major General Zavorin watched the Mossad chief disappear down
the paved pathway. The Colonel's leaving Israel signified an important operation. According to East German Intelligence his
meeting here, with Fleske, meant they were planning to kill the
boy. Zavorin would stop them.

Though the Colonel's movements would ordinarily demand
primary attention, the Russian didn't follow him. His interest at
the moment was Fleske. Zavorin felt reasonably confident that the
CIA agent would lead him to Steve Barth.

May 20
The Previous
Spring

Two-Moscow

KGB Colonel Petr Dmitrivich Grigorenko hurried through the light green corridors of the Dzerzhinsky Square complex known as the Center. Passing from the gray stone structure, enclosing the courtyard that faced the infamous Lubyanka Prison, into the newer nine-story addition constructed by political prisoners and captured German soldiers after World War II, Grigorenko entered the section of KGB headquarters housing the First Chief Directorate. He asked to see Alexandr Zavorin and was quickly ushered from the harsh, globe-illuminated reception area into the department chief's chambers.

Zavorin's office was a large, broad room with mahogany paneled walls, rich Oriental carpets, patterned sofas, a high ceiling, and tall windows overlooking the square on Marx Prospekt. Adjoining the office was a private shower and toilet. A portrait of "Iron Felix" Dzerzhinsky, the Polish revolutionary and founding director of the Cheka, as the secret police had been called after the Revolution, hung behind Zavorin's head. Across from it stood a picture of Pavlik Morozov, Hero of the Soviet Union, who was lynched by enraged peasants in 1932. Defying the law, Pavlik's father had given refuge to land-owning peasants dispossessed by Stalin's attempt at collectivization. At the age of fourteen Pavlik, an idealistic Soviet youth, informed on his father, who was shot.

Colonel Petr Grigorenko crossed Zavorin's thick carpet and was unpleasantly reminded of his stark Fifth Directorate cubicle, with its forty-year-old desk, assembly-line chairs, and small, greasy windows that couldn't be cleaned because of the bars over them. Between his desk and the safe he sealed with wax nightly was a passageway, so narrow that, although he was short and exceedingly thin, he had to squeeze through it in order to reach his chair. He resented Zavorin but tried to console himself with the fact that the Fifth Chief Directorate, established by the Politburo in 1969 to erase political dissent and reinforce controls over the general population, was relatively new and had only begun to prove itself.

Grigorenko, at forty-two, was on his way up. Chosen to head the Jewish Department when it was established in 1971, he had been singularly successful at halting public protests, recruiting Jewish informants, and infiltrating trained agents into dissident circles. Late in 1972 he had even managed to force suspension of the underground *Chronicle of Current Events*, whose accurate reporting infuriated the Kremlin. Grigorenko had compiled a random list of intellectuals whom he promised to imprison if another issue of the *Chronicle* appeared. Out of compassion for the innocent, the sponsors of the journal suspended publication. Yet, despite these successes, Colonel Grigorenko's rank and status remained unchanged. Sometimes, he wondered if the stain associated with Jews had rubbed off on him.

Zavorin invited Grigorenko to sit. A graduate of the Second Kiev Artillery School, the Frunze Military Academy, and the Dzerzhinsky Engineering Military Academy, Zavorin was an ex-GRU army officer who ran secret service operations as if they were war games. He'd come to Khrushchev's attention in the uncertain period after Stalin's death and because he was military and not publicly political he'd survived the transition to Brezhnev's reign. Ruthless and unbending, he was violently opposed to detente with the United States.

"I'm glad you could come so promptly, Colonel," Zavorin said.

"The Major General intimated that it was important." Grigorenko sank into the soft chair in the center of the room.

"As you know, the Collegium must present its yearly operational plan to the Politburo before July 1." The seams and lines in the soft flesh around Zavorin's blue eyes tightened. "I am preparing my report now and I would like to include the fact that Operation Cloverleaf has been set in motion."

"But we agreed to wait another year," Grigorenko protested. "I want to let my man work himself deeper into Zionist circles." He despised the burden of a binding master plan that saddled officers and agents with production quotas and enormously counterproductive pressures.

"Originally we had." Zavorin smiled sympathetically. "But I would not like the expulsion of more than a hundred of our people from Great Britain to remain without an appropriate response."

Grigorenko stared at the portrait of the child Morozov, anger burrowing inside him. The hundred and five KGB and GRU agents had been expelled from England three years ago! They had nothing to do with Cloverleaf: the code name for the plan to activate the Soviet sleeper agents in the West. It was absurd pushing up a major operation to slap at the British, after so long. Besides, England would suffer little from the consequences of Cloverleaf. Grigorenko suspected that Zavorin, responsible for all clandestine activities abroad, was in difficulty and needed an immediate success to ingratiate himself with the Politburo.

"How soon do you plan to activate the sleepers in Israel?" Grigorenko asked, his voice flat. He was powerless to fight Zavorin.

"Actually, I would like you to take a message to our operative in London as soon as possible. We need a young foreigner, preferably an American who speaks Hebrew, sent to Moscow. Someone who will return to Israel, that's imperative. He will work for us without realizing it *and* without drawing the attention a Soviet Jew would."

"I know," Grigorenko snapped. He had created Cloverleaf; he didn't need this bourgeois bureaucrat explaining his own operation.

Zavorin, registering his subordinate's tone and filing it away, continued. "The boy can be sent under the pretext that the underground Hebrew teachers here need advanced texts. It seems, suddenly, that there's a shortage of instruction materials in Moscow." Zavorin opened the mahogany door to the cabinet behind him, scooped up several piles of books, and dropped them across the desk. "My men attended some of their classes this week," he said, laughing.

At the sight of the Hebrew texts, smuggled into the Soviet Union by tourists over a period of years, Grigorenko too began to laugh.

"Take them," Zavorin said loudly, waving one hand over the books. "Decorate the walls of the Jewish department. Save the pages for the next toilet paper shortage."

Grigorenko grabbed an armful of the books, piling them against his chest. But there were too many; he couldn't hold them.

"Stop, stop." Zavorin laughed louder. "I'll get someone to bring them up to you."

Grigorenko dropped the books on the desk.

"Is there anything else?" he asked, moving toward the door.

"Just one thing. Our operative in London has been placed among the Zionists with the utmost difficulty. His cover must not be jeopardized. Under any circumstances. Do you understand?"

"Yes."

Grigorenko turned and left the room, anger rippling through him.

Three-Jerusalem

Steve Barth pitched restlessly under the stiff sheets. The dream wrapped its tentacles around him again, squeezing. He dug his fingers into the pillow. A shot. Screams.

Sweating, Steve woke. He tried to lie still, not wanting to wake the dark-haired girl sleeping on the far edge of the bed. He couldn't. He had to move, get out. Placing one foot on the linoleum floor he inched from under the covers; the cold air slapped his body. He reached for his clothes draped over a folding chair. His belt buckle rattled, scraping the silence.

Memories rolled through him like an avalanche. Running.

The cry of the crowd. *Let me through. Hey, J. R.* Noise. You, get the hell back. What do you think you're doing? Keep in line. Stop him—hey, no pushing. We're going to keep this nonviolent. *J. R.!* Shoving into the crowd. Somebody grab that guy. Breaking through. In the open, almost there . . . Sound of a gunshot. Bending over the body. Blood on his hands.

If he'd arrived a few seconds earlier. His fault. *If only I hadn't stopped for breakfast.* . . .

Steve looked at Dahlia. Her breathing remained slow and even. He wondered what she'd feel when she woke and found him gone: anger, sadness, affection? He despised the fact that women were attracted to his indifference, his inaccessibility. It seemed an aberration, a conspiracy to keep him from caring. If he couldn't care, he didn't want them to.

Steve took a last glance at the figure curled around the pillow. She gave to him so selflessly and asked so little in return, but he couldn't provide even that.

Outside, the sun edged above the Hills of Edom setting the city below aglow. The odors of the day were unformed, the air clean. From Mount Scopus Steve walked down Derech Shechem, through a segmented valley where sheep grazed near a shepherd, silhouetted on a rock. Shadowy hills lined the horizon. In the clefts of the rocks of the valley wild cyclamens pushed up through a blaze of anemones.

A stiff-tailed cat raced across the street, and sprang up the trunk of a tree to its uppermost leaves. Safe, she peered down, bristling and hissing scornfully. A fresh wind rose, rolling through the valley. Steve continued toward the university.

The Givat Ram campus was a long stretch of grass, bordered

on the west by low, attached classroom buildings and surrounded by a chain-link fence. A guard at the front gate pawed through Steve's bags before he was allowed to enter.

Steve walked toward Popick Hall. Iron letters on the facade of the building announced that Rita and Jack Popick of Miami had endowed construction of the building for the Humanities. By attaching their names to their offering the Popicks, though probably unaware of it, dropped to a pale fourth on Maimonides's hierarchical degrees of charity. The donators' plaques rife on the campus embarrassed Steve. Shortly after arriving he had taken the formica strip, thanking Herman and Ethel Bloomenfeld, off the wall next to his dorm door and relocated it in the communal bathroom, directly over the toilets.

Entering Professor Aryeh Ben Tor's Introduction to Mediterranean Archaeology, Steve took an end seat and watched with disinterest as slides flashed on the screen at the front of the room. He recognized only two: a photo of the bath house atop Massada and another of the jars that held the Qumran scrolls. The professor droned his descriptions rapidly, just above a whisper. After a year at the Hebrew University Steve finally understood the language, but found he liked the lectures better before he did. At the moment Professor Ben Tor was holding a review session; the final was a week away. Steve had devoted little attention to the course and it seemed pointless to review something he knew nothing about. Besides, what difference would it make if he could differentiate between Greek and Roman influence on Second Temple Period structures? For that matter, what difference did anything make?

A bright flash of white abruptly filled the space where the last slide had been. Ben Tor snapped on the overhead lights and along with seventy-five other bodies Barth rose and moved toward the door.

"It's going to be a tough exam. He covered a lot of material," a sandy-haired student said to Steve in English as they squeezed outside.

"Yeah." Steve headed for the gates.

"Have you studied much?" he asked, remaining close.

"Nope."

"Then maybe I could help you. I have a pretty good background in archaeology."

"Why bother?"

"What?" He frowned.

"I said I couldn't care less if I know anything about Mediterranean Archaeology."

"Then how come you're in the course?"

Steve stopped walking. "The average student around here has nine finals. How come you want to help me?"

"I just think Americans ought to help each other. It's pretty tough competing with the Israelis in their language."

"I see," Steve said, although he didn't.

"My name's Mark Abrams." The young man held out his hand.

"Steve Barth."

"Nice to meet you, Steve." Abrams felt a firm, dry grip. "Look, if you're not in a hurry why don't we get some coffee and bring it out on the grass. I want to enjoy this weather before it gets too hot."

"Okay."

A few minutes later, styrofoam cups in hand, they settled on the ground near a grove of pines, their needles rustling in the warm wind.

"How long have you been in Israel?" Abrams asked.

"About a year."

"Do you like it?"

"Sometimes more, sometimes less."

"Things have gone pretty well for me here," Abrams volunteered. "But at the moment I can't decide if I should travel across Europe on my way home or stay and work on a kibbutz. I keep changing my mind. How about you? You staying through the summer?"

Steve shrugged. "Maybe."

"You sound bored."

No response.

"What are you doing after finals?"

"Not much."

"If I was to offer you a free trip to London including food and a place to stay, what would you say?"

"What do I have to do?"

"Talk to a few people."

"About what?" Steve asked coldly.

"Russia." Abrams took a slow sip from his cup. "They're in contact with Jews there."

"So, what does that have to do with me?"

"They arrange for people to travel to the Soviet Union."

"Why?"

"To make contact with the underground movement in Moscow."

The coffee left an unpleasant taste in Steve's mouth. He

emptied the liquid remaining in his cup into the bushes. "Why approach me?"

"No particular reason. I thought you might be interested."

"Don't give me that shit. Why me?"

"Well," Abrams said, "you look like a typical American: blond, blue eyes, a red beard."

"You mean I don't look Jewish. What else?"

"Your name, Barth . . ."

"Changed from Berkowitz, 'for the kid's sake,' " Steve said sarcastically. "Go on."

"The rare comments you make in class have been intelligent, you seem to know how to handle yourself, and you speak Hebrew."

Steve nodded, beginning now to understand. "What's in this for me?"

"A free trip—all expenses paid to London, into Russia, and back to Jerusalem."

"What? No rusty Haganah medal or pat on the head from Golda?"

Abrams rose abruptly. "Okay, friend, forget the whole thing. We'll find someone else."

"Wait a second," Steve said, jumping up. "I was kidding. Tell me more about it. I have nothing better to do."

The Colonel peered past President's Park into the Valley of the Cross. Opening the sliding glass window, he listened to the carillons of the belfry, partially visible above the Monastery's high walls. Tradition had it that the sixth-century structure covered the spot where the tree used to make the cross for the crucifixion of

Christ once stood. And tradition was a potent force in the Middle East—whether as ally or adversary.

A light rap sounded in the hall. The Colonel crossed the room, and slowly pulled the door open. "Mark Abrams," he said, ushering the young man into his office. "Sit down and tell me what happened." Abrams, a native-born American who had emigrated to Israel with his parents, was one of the Colonel's most promising new agents.

"I think he's perfect," Abrams said, dropping into a cushioned chair. "Evidently Berkeley burned him out. He got picked up for some unpaid parking tickets and while waiting in the station overheard the police planning to get rid of a student protest leader named Johnny Robinson. Barth found out where he lived and tried to warn him. He waited outside his apartment for hours that night, then left a note on his door explaining it was urgent Robinson call. Robinson either didn't get the message or was too busy to answer it. There was a big demonstration scheduled for the following day. Barth grabbed breakfast in the dorms, then tried Robinson's apartment again. The neighbors explained that he'd already left for the demonstration. Barth ran the entire way. He was only a few yards from Robinson when the bullet hit, seconds too late. He blamed himself, convinced that if he hadn't stopped for breakfast he would have saved him." Abrams paused, then took a breath. "He turned himself off. I don't think we'll have to worry about his reacting emotionally inside Russia."

"Excellent," the Colonel said, lighting a Montecruz cigar. "Our friends in London will be pleased. It's nice to be able to help them out; they've done a lot for us. You'd be amazed at the quality of the intelligence they've turned up. Absolutely first rate. And without the use of a government base."

"I've heard they have quite an operation going," Abrams said, noncommittally. He had been warned that the Colonel never volunteered information gratuitously, so he waited for the older man to work his way toward what he wanted.

"Mark, you know, I was thinking about the operation London requested." The Colonel flicked a tip of ash into his wastebasket. "It's going to be pretty tough for Barth, alone in Russia. I was wondering if we should find some girl to accompany him. Besides, it might look less suspicious if he wasn't traveling by himself." The chair squeaked as the Colonel pushed back from his desk. "Tell me, you're about his age. What do you think? Would you feel more comfortable if you had a girl along?"

"That depends on the girl. If she was pleasant and reasonably attractive, I'd like it better than going alone."

"Would Barth?"

"Probably . . . but I'm not sure." Abrams hesitated. "It sounds like a good idea," he added uncomfortably.

"Then take care of it for me, Mark. We have an agent in London, Joseph Eliav, who runs Westworld Travel and Tours in Russell Square. I'd like you to pay him a visit. Tell him I suggest he find a girl to send along with Barth, someone to keep the boy company. He'll handle everything from there." The Colonel rose. Moving around the desk, he wrapped his arm around Abrams's shoulder. "And enjoy yourself. Catch a few shows in the West End while you're in London."

"I will." Abrams managed a smile and headed toward the door.

"Oh, one last thing," the Colonel said. "You might ask Eliav to get in touch with me."

"Okay."

After Abrams left the room the Colonel dialed Operational Planning. Yehuda Shamir answered almost immediately.

"Yehuda, I'd like you to contact Moscow Center," the Colonel said, leaning forward in his chair.

"Yes."

"I want *Pravda*'s obituary pages sent to me daily."

"Need anything else?"

The Colonel breathed into the receiver. "You'd better cable me the daily soccer scores too."

"Did you say soccer scores?" The Old Man's crazy, Shamir thought to himself. What does he want those for?

"You understood me correctly, Yehuda. Please get on it as soon as possible."

"I will." About to hang up, Shamir suddenly changed his mind. "Colonel." He hesitated, then plunged into what was worrying him. "We've got to locate those Soviet sleeper agents soon."

"I know," the Colonel said. "That's what I'm working on."

Four-London

As the El Al plane flew over the fishing village of Trouville and crossed the Normandy coastline, Steve peered out the window. In the English Channel crests of waves, white, slapped at the soft sea. A string of toy boats were heading home in the remaining evening light. Steve stretched and kicked off one shoe. The air conditioning, escaping a floor vent, felt cold against his moist sock.

His mind wandered back to Berkeley: four years of tear gas choking besieged streets, of students more desperate than angry—lashing out, begging to be taken seriously, shattering windows in frustration. After the first year of fun and experimenting, suddenly with the second September he and his friends pitched precariously on the lip of a gaping abyss. "Who am I? Where am I? Why am I?" they asked desperately. Some tried to find themselves through sex and sensual stimulation, others grasped onto the Maharishi and meditation, the more conventional turned to Jesus and Judaism. And of course there were drugs. Impatient, what they really wanted was a pill or prophet that could give them the answers they longed for.

Finally when tear gas became *the* response to their questions and the invasion of Cambodia proved the futility of dissent, they turned inward, and stopped caring. The student movement was over.

After Johnny Robinson's death Steve had grown quiet, distant. In cafeterias, lecture halls, libraries he chose to sit by himself. He preferred privacy. His friends tried to persuade him that he'd done everything he could. He wouldn't listen. He wouldn't return their calls. After a while they stopped phoning. . . .

The plane dropped into a floor of clouds, and the landing gear kicked down. Ears clogging, Steve swallowed and looked outside. A gray-white wave of fog rolled against the window. Then suddenly London became visible: red tile roofs, stretches of green, the spires of Parliament, the muddy serpentine Thames.

Moments later the plane banged down on the runway, bounced, then slowed with the application of the engines' reverse thrust. When the Israeli airliner rolled to a halt Steve rose and reached for the Levi jacket he'd tossed into the compartment above his head. Walking down the steep steps, he noticed that the plane's engines, which should have been shut down by now, still whined furiously. Inside the pilot's compartment everyone remained in place. As he hurried into the damp evening, Steve realized that the plane, if attacked by Arab terrorists, was ready to move.

At passport control the immigration officer looked at the blond, bearded youth and asked him to produce evidence of means to leave the country. Steve reached into the small day pack slung over his shoulder and pulled out a creased and wrinkled return ticket, noticing that those better dressed passed through the booths on either side of him without delay. The clerk mumbled something about the number of kids stranded in England each summer and stamped a standard six-month tourist visa in Steve's passport.

A customs matron passed through the stream of tired passengers and, moving her arm, summoned Steve for a spot check. He lowered his backpack onto her table and watched impassively as she struggled with the knots. Finally, she began to remove his articles of clothing. After finding only a layer of paperback novels at the bottom of the nylon pack, she replaced his clothes. He watched her, silent, his stomach taut. She searched the side pouches, then waved him on.

Outside he hailed a cab and gave the driver an address in Whitechapel. Though Steve had never been to London he had no curiosity about the English countryside. As the driver sped east on the M4 motorway he dozed.

The taxi jerked to a halt in front of a row of two-story terraced houses on Sidney Street. Steve groggily removed his glasses and rubbed both eyes. The cool evening arched a chill through his body. As the cab sped away Steve stared at the high brick facade of the Watney Manns Brewery across the street, remembering from some long-forgotten source that Jack the Ripper had prowled this area of London.

Steve passed through a low iron gate and knocked at number seventeen. Rock music and the clatter of voices sounded within. Steve doubted that his rapping could be heard, so he tried the door, which opened. As he entered a narrow, thickly carpeted hall, a man appeared at an interior door. He was tall and powerfully built with long brown hair, styled and brushed over his ears, flowing onto a tapered shirt. His left wrist was in a cast.

"You must be Steve," he said with a warm smile.

"Yes."

"I'm Michael Marks . . . Mike. Glad to meet you. How was the flight?"

"Fine," Steve said.

"Dynamite." Mike lifted the backpack from the floor. "Come on, I'll take you to your room. If you're tired you can rest."

"I slept in the cab," Steve said, following him up narrow, steep stairs.

The small room contained a double bed, dresser, and desk. The cream-colored walls were bare, the open closet empty.

"There's a bit of a party going on downstairs," Mike said, standing the pack against the closet door. "If you like, come down and enjoy yourself."

Before Steve could respond he was gone.

Music beat through the small house. Steve sat on the bed and leaned against the wall, feeling the vibrations in his back. His collar was damp but he didn't feel like changing his shirt or unpacking. And he didn't feel like a party. He hated parties, with their artificial, affected conversation. But in a few minutes, he got up and went downstairs.

The main room, small with knotted-pine-paneled walls, was dim, the light from the corner lamps barely cutting through the haze of cigarette smoke. A bar next to a gas fireplace dispensed drinks. Glasses, empty and half-filled, were scattered over its white formica counter. The guests, sprawled on sofas and chatting loudly, paid no attention to Steve's entrance.

"I'm Vicki, Mike's wife. Come, let me get you something to drink," a woman said, touching Steve's arm and guiding him toward the bar. "What'll you have?" She was tall and attractive, wearing short streaked hair and a clinging, low-cut blouse.

Steve searched the top of the counter for the beer that wasn't there. "How about a screwdriver with an extra shot of orange juice?"

Laughing softly, she poured his drink. "Now let me introduce you to a few of our friends. Cindy, Laurie," she called to a cluster of young people standing a few feet away. "Come meet our American guest."

"Hi," one of the girls said, moving close. "Have you been in England long?"

"I arrived this evening," Steve said, wondering if getting laid came with the plane ticket. "I just met Mike a few minutes ago."

"He's a great guy."

"Yeah, I guess so," Steve said hesitantly. "What's your name? I'm sorry, I didn't catch it."

"Cindy." She tossed her hair behind her head.

"Would you like to dance?" he asked, so he wouldn't have to talk.

"Sure."

The hours brushed into each other and fell away. The music pounded relentlessly. Steve danced, drank too much, and listened to stories that bored him. Sometime after eleven, spotting Mike sunk into the sofa talking to another man, he inched away from a nameless girl, whose conversation contained suggestive reference to a vacationing roommate. I'm not on the make, he thought tiredly, threading his way across the room. I didn't come here for that.

"I was bloody lucky to get away with only a broken wrist," Mike was saying to the other, apparently too engrossed in conversation to notice Steve.

"It could have been much worse," the man responded. "Do you know who did it?"

Mike shrugged. "Take your pick. Russians, Arabs."

"But sawing through the axle of your car, that's a bit dodgy. Your kids could have been killed."

"Luckily I banged into that gate. It broke the impact." He rubbed the outside of his cast. "I don't know, sometimes I wonder why we continue. It's been a bloody difficult year."

Steve listened with irritation. Why fly him to England then ignore him?

"Excuse me," he said, coughing self-consciously.

"Steve." Mike sat forward as if noticing him for the first time. "I'm glad you found me. I was just thinking that we might go upstairs and talk."

The boy nodded.

In Steve's room Mike lowered himself carefully into a folding chair. A second man entered and closed the door behind him. He was fiftyish, of medium height, with a sack of flesh hanging over his waist. His bald pate was surrounded by a hedge of blond hair. "Steve, this is David. David, Steve."

Steve gripped the man's hand.

"Mike has told me about you, and let me say that we're glad to have you with us," David said, easing himself into the upholstered chair by the door. "Everything all right in Israel?"

"The country's about the same, I guess."

"You finished school with no problems?"

"No serious ones."

"Good." To Steve's amazement David placed his hands on the arms of the chair, pushed himself up, and turned to Mike. "I'm a bit tired tonight. You'll excuse me if I leave the party early. I'm getting old, you know." Mike laughed. "Nice meeting you," David said, turning to Steve. Then he left the room.

Mike rose. "If you want, you can turn in. Otherwise come back down and enjoy yourself. I think a couple of our young friends rather fancied you."

"I think I'll just stay here," Steve said.

"As you like."

"Could you close the door on your way out?"

"Of course."

As the door shut Steve slammed his fist into the pillow. What was this? Who were these people? What did they expect him to do—bring one of those girls up here and screw her? And this David—why hadn't he said anything? He seemed so disinterested. What the hell was going on?

Steve peeled off his clothes and threw them on the floor. He was tired and sweaty. It had been humid in Tel Aviv and there was a two-hour time difference—two A.M. in Israel now. Deciding against a shower, he pulled back the blankets, thrust himself underneath them, and courted sleep. The minutes clung to each other. A sliver of lightning flashed outside the window followed by a roll of thunder. There was a loud silence, then rain began to drum against the glass pane. Trying not to think, he lay still for a long time, staring at the ceiling, listening to the rain.

Five-London

Steve woke, shaken by a nightmare. As he grabbed at the images trying to hold them, they moved away, fading out of reach—he was left only with the sensation of having had a bad dream. Immediately he pushed himself out of the bed, knowing if he lingered, even for a minute, he'd be trapped there, unable to move.

Downstairs all traces of the previous night's party had disappeared. In the kitchen Steve found Mike and Vicki sitting at the small corner table, sipping tea.

"Would you like some eggs on toast?" Vicki asked.

"Please."

The splattering of an egg frying in oil filled the silence. Above the noise Steve heard the sound of the front door opening. Seconds later a short, powerfully built man wearing a T-shirt that did not begin to hide his muscles or tattoos sauntered into the kitchen.

"What's up, guv'ner?" he asked Mike.

"Not much. I want you to meet Steve, a new friend of ours. Steve, Wulf."

"Fantastic." Wulf slapped Steve's shoulder warmly. "Glad to 'ave you with us."

"What happened last night?" Mike asked. "We were expecting you."

"Couldn't make it, guv'ner, lost me screwdriver." Wulf's lips curved into a smile. "You see, I was driving round Gants 'ill when this fella in a beat-up van stalls in front of me. In a bit of a 'urry to get to the party I tooted 'im. Well, apparently the geeser gets the needle for 'e stops the van and jumps out. A right big bloke 'e was. 'e comes up and yells you God damn dirty Jewish cunt, and takes a swipe at me right through the window. So I leans back, grabs me screwdriver, and sticks it clean through the geeser's 'and. Scream 'e did. It was beautiful. I guess 'e thinks everybody what lives in Ilford are timid little Jews with Ghetto mentalities. 'e pulls the screwdriver out and flings it into the bushes, the blood gushing. Then just me luck a copper comes up because the traffic's stalled, nicks me, and takes me to the station. Inside 'e makes me take off all me rings and jewelry then the geeser goes for me Jewish Star. I start screaming and yelling: 'You may as well cut off me bleedin' legs, but let me 'ave me Star of David.' I was making so much noise 'e let me keep it. A little while later this chap comes into the cell with some pork pies and chips. I reach out to take them but then I think I better act disgusted. I tells the geeser I ain't allowed to eat that stuff, I'm a Jew. I points to the chips and I says, ''ow do I know they ain't fried in pig's fat?' 'e takes it away and comes back 'alf an 'our later with two salt beef sandwiches and lemon tea. And you *know* I 'ate lemon tea. About fifteen minutes after that the patrolman who nicked me 'auls me before the sergeant. The patrolman's a real 'ospitable bloke. 'e tells me 'e didn't want to nick me but that's 'is job. But the sergeant's a tough bastard. 'e says an old man and woman was walking across the street. They 'eard the geeser in the van calling me insulting names, and saw 'im 'ave a go at me first. The sergeant tells me: 'I ain't giving you no license to stick screwdrivers into people, but I ain't 'olding 'im and I ain't 'olding you, so go on piss out of 'ere.' " Wulf shrugged his shoulders. "Can you believe the way the coppers talk these days."

Mike laughed. Steve ate his breakfast in silence, waiting for these men to initiate a conversation about Russia.

"Why don't you move into the living room so I can clean up," Vicki suggested, after they'd finished eating. "I'll fix some tea and bring it in."

Steve sat on the couch next to Wulf. "I'd like to ask some questions about Russia. This guy Mark Abrams said . . ."

"You don't have to concern yourself with that now," Mike interrupted. "I expect David this afternoon, he'll speak to you then. In the meantime we'll have a little chat, take you on a tour of London, and by the time we return I'm sure David will be here. Does that sound okay with you?"

"I guess so."

"Why'd you decide to go to Israel?" Wulf asked.

Steve shrugged. "I wish I could say I went to Israel because I was a Zionist or going there had been a lifelong dream, but that's not so. I was just fed up with what I was doing. I didn't want to go to law school, I didn't want to work at some meaningless job, and I was bored sitting around doing nothing. I met a professor in Los Angeles, talked to him for a while and he suggested I try Israel. He made all the arrangements for me, so I went. If I would've met someone who offered to take me to France, I would just as soon have gone there." He told that story so often he almost believed it.

Later, Mike and Vicki took him on the promised tour of London. They traveled over, around, and on the Thames. After lunch his hosts walked him through Buckingham Palace, the Tate Gallery, Westminster Abbey, and several other required spots. The three of them were thoroughly bored.

Moments after Steve settled back into Mike's living room, a glass of red burgundy in his hand, there was a knock at the door. David entered.

"Sorry we didn't have much of a chance to chat last night," David said, settling deeply into the sofa. "I was a bit tired."

"His young lady's been wearing him out," Mike teased.

David smiled, masking his face, and turned toward Steve. "Your flight from Tel Aviv was smooth?"

"Yes," Steve said, trying to mute the frustration in his voice.

"School went well?"

Steve nodded.

"You had no trouble adjusting to the time change?"

"None."

"Well, then," David said, crossing one leg over the other. "I understand you want to go to Russia." Like last night, he had been testing the boy's frustration level, monitoring how he reacted to the arbitrary—the type of treatment he would face in Russia, if caught.

"Yes." Steve responded cautiously, sensing that every syllable spoken to this man was filed, to be recalled and exploited at will.

"We have an independent tour booked for you," David said. "It leaves for the Soviet Union on Friday. You will remain there one week. You are being sent to bring special textbooks to the underground Hebrew teachers in Moscow."

"For some reason the KGB suddenly decided to crack down on the Hebrew classes," Mike explained in a friendlier tone. "In a series of coordinated sweeps they succeeded in confiscating a large number of their instruction books. It's imperative that the supply be replenished immediately, before the movement is weakened."

David reached in his coat pocket for his pipe, filled and lit it. "What we are asking you to do is important. But we warn you it may be dangerous. If you don't want to go we fully understand. You owe us nothing; the trip from Israel to London will remain at our expense. The only thing I can tell you is that if for any reason you are detained or arrested we will make every effort within human possibility to get you out. If you want to know how this will be accomplished you may ask Mike after I leave. Well," he said, sucking on the pipe. "Are you still interested?"

David stared into Steve's eyes, as if able to judge the boy's steadiness by the amount of time elapsed before he diverted his gaze. Steve greeted his stare stubbornly. "Yes," he said. "I'm interested." At least, if only for a week, I won't be bored, he thought.

"You have Israel stamped in your passport, I assume," David said.

"I have a student visa."

41

David rose slowly, shuffling his heavy frame toward Steve. "Let me see it."

Steve stuck his hand into his pants pocket.

"Give me your glass," David said.

Steve handed him his passport and the wine. Without a word the round man moved toward the kitchen. He returned momentarily holding the passport in a damp napkin, and handed it to Steve. Red burgundy had been spilled over the pages. "First thing in the morning go to the American Embassy and tell them somebody knocked wine over it at a party. I have not stained the pages which contain your vital statistics so they will not suspect tampering." He pulled a five-pound note from his wallet and placed it on the table. "This should cover the cost of a new passport. Do you have some photographs?"

Steve nodded.

"Good. After you finish with the Americans you'll have to go to the Russian Embassy and get your visa. They will want two photographs. Your tour is already booked, but we could not apply for a Russian visa without your new passport number. It's a mere formality. If you show them the voucher for the tour you should have the visa in forty-eight hours."

"I see."

"We want you to enjoy yourself tonight. Starting tomorrow we will have certain suggestions to make, photographs for you to study, and of course there will be some information for you to memorize. The books will be brought here Thursday night. You will deliver them to a man named Zev Zaretsky; you will give them to no one else. Mike will explain later. And one more thing." David bent and knocked the tobacco from his pipe into an ashtray. "You'll be traveling with a girl. Her name is Susan Stern. She was at the party last night. Short, brunette, attractive, I'm sure you remember her. It would look suspicious for a young man to be traveling in Russia alone. Since you went to Berkeley let us say that you two became interested in leftist politics there. It is quite logical, she's an American. I will leave you, Susan, and Mike to work out the details of your past. I'll try and be back before you leave. If I can't make it, best of luck and I'll see you when you return." He did not discuss the danger that faced the young couple or mention that the threat to their lives could strike from more than one side.

As David ambled toward the door Steve tried to remember if he'd talked to anyone named Susan. But last night's names and faces were a blur. A short brunette. He'd met a brunette early in the evening, before he'd started drinking. He reached for the empty glass of wine standing next to his passport and cupped it in his hand. What difference did it make who she was?

"Would you like a refill?" Mike asked, studying the boy.

Steve shook his head. "David mentioned something about options in the event I'm arrested. Do you think you could . . ."

Just then the doorbell rang.

"Excuse me," Mike said. He returned seconds later with a young woman Steve didn't remember having seen the night before. Slim, wearing an open blouse that didn't fully cover small, braless breasts, she nodded to Steve, with a smile. Her skin was deeply tanned; her brown hair, long. The light cotton pants she wore fit snugly against taut buttocks. She looked in her early twenties.

"Steve, I'd like you to meet Susan Stern, your traveling companion."

"Hello." He didn't get up.

"Hi," she said quietly.

"I thought you two might want to get acquainted," Mike said.

"I've been looking forward to meeting you." She hitched her leather purse higher on her shoulder. "Would you like to go out for a drink? There's a pub nearby. We could talk."

He watched her. She was attractive—for what that was worth. "If you'd like," he said.

"Well, come on then."

He pushed himself to his feet and followed her out the door.

Low, leaden clouds blanketed the sky. Susan led him quickly along Whitechapel Road across from the blackened brick facade of London Hospital. Wooden stalls crowded with vegetables, fruit, flowers, clothes, and records lined the gray slab sidewalk. Buddy Holly, Diana Ross, and Porter Wagoner tunes poured from crackling speakers, all for sale. Lace, colored, and patterned bras flapped in the wind next to rows of orange jockey shorts, the British flag, and the mocking challenge: STAND UP FOR BRITAIN printed across each crotch. Past the underground station, outside Joe Coral Ltd. Turf Accountants, a man sat on an empty milk crate, a thin hand-rolled cigarette drooping from his mouth. He wore a green tweed coat ragged at the elbows. A two-day-old salt-and-pepper beard bristled from his face. Inside, several men, hunched over, holding unfiltered cigarettes in their stained fingers, filled out racing forms, glancing occasionally at the results scratched on the blackboard running along the far wall. Rumpled and torn scraps of bookmaker's bet slips lay strewn on the floor.

The Star and Garter Saloon Bar was dim and sparsely peopled. The top third of the windows running along the walls was dark red, the middle third clear, and the lower section blotted by black vinyl drapes. A faded red patterned carpet covered the floor and red felt wallpaper, with dark pinwheels raised against a pink background, adorned the remaining walls.

Steve and Susan ordered half pints of Skol lager and settled across from each other at a low wooden table near the bar.

"I wish they had nuts in these pubs," Susan said, sipping her beer. "If people only ate nuts and organic vegetables they'd never need glasses."

Steve adjusted his wireframes self-consciously. "Is that so?"

"Sure. What about you? Do you eat nuts and organic vegetables?"

Steve gulped down half his glass. "No."

"I should have gotten to you earlier."

He smiled. "And what do you do when you're not eating nuts and vegetables?"

"Yoga," she said, putting down a third of her beer in one long drink. "Usually forty-five minutes each morning and evening."

He went to the bar and ordered two full pints of lager.

"In between the yoga I'm at the London School of Contemporary Dance," she added. "I used to be in modern dance at Radcliffe but I didn't like it there. They spent too much time teaching us how to pivot and pirouette sexually. In the first six months I learned how to dance intercourse in thirteen positions. It was rather tedious. So I tried the real thing with the teacher, liked it, and flew to London."

"What's the connection between liking it and flying to London?"

"None."

Steve drained his first glass and started on the second.

Susan took another long drink, then pushed her near empty

mug across the table leaving a damp trail on the polished wood. "Why do you want to go to Russia?" she asked.

"Because I'm bored."

"I see." She took the full pint mug and held the cold glass between her fingers. "What sign are you?"

"I'm not sure, Taurus or Gemini, I get confused."

"When's your birthday?"

"May seventeenth."

"Taurus." Her eyes expressed concern. "That may be a problem."

"A problem?"

"Yes. I'm a Libra. Libras and Tauruses are Venus ruled. That's a difficult combination—particularly for the Taurus."

He laughed. "Come on. You don't really believe that crap." Lifting the mug to his mouth, he let a large quantity of beer race down his throat. "You think my birth date can tell you something about me?"

"Of course. Astrology is scientific. Tauruses take things too much to heart, are stubborn, suffer from self-censorship, guilt, and usually keep complaints and frustrations locked inside. Consequently they are prone to constriction ailments—laryngitis, stuttering, constipation."

Steve's face fell. "That's ridiculous."

Susan read the taut lines around his mouth and eyes and checked herself.

"Let me tell you why I want to go to Russia," she volunteered, changing the subject. "When I was at Radcliffe I used to go out with this guy named Paul Schiffer. He was working with this fantastic group called the Student Struggle for Soviet Jewry. He convinced me to take a trip to Moscow, Leningrad, and Kiev with him in the summer. I was really excited about going but after a few months I began to realize he was trying to make a hero out of himself by 'saving' Soviet Jews. He became obsessed with the subject, irrational. He'd flare into tantrums. Though I still loved him, after a while I lost trust in his judgment. A week before we were scheduled to leave I cancelled my reservation." She looked at Steve, seeing the hardness in his eyes. "I still want to go to Russia. Mike told me he thought I could trust you. Now that we've met I feel he was right."

Her candor surprised him; Steve never would have been so open with a stranger. "I'm flattered," he said self-consciously. Despite himself he was beginning to like her.

Draining his mug, he ordered another pint from the bartender. Solitary men lined the walls, smoking, their silence broken by occasional wheezing coughs. One man, his black hair combed back, purple-red veins puffed on his nose, stared at the floor, a bottle of ale held loosely by the tips of his fingers.

Steve went back to his table and turned to Susan. "I haven't thought about our trip much but when I was in college I was fascinated by Russian and German history," he said, the beer he had drunk crumbling the shell surrounding him. "Particularly World War Two. I read everything about the Nazis I could get my hands on. I was obsessed by the wholesale destruction of people, by mass murder without remorse. I can't understand why the world seems to *need* to forget. Nobody wants to remember . . . except the Jews and the Russians."

"I don't know much about history," Susan said, leaving her drink untouched. "Were many Russians killed in the war?"

"Were many Russians killed," Steve repeated, incredulously. "Twenty million people died on the Eastern front. Twenty

47

million! Most of them froze or starved to death. Hitler really cornered the market on the elements. Those he couldn't freeze he burned into smoke. And who gives a shit? Nobody. There are hundreds of former Nazis living in Europe and the United States, today. Nobody does a fucking thing about it." He grabbed at his glass and angrily gulped the rest of the beer.

Suddenly the greasy fish and chips he'd had for lunch began to move. He bolted for the door marked w.c., thought for a moment he was all right, then retched in the direction of a seatless toilet. An acrid smell stung his nostrils. Sweating and simultaneously trembling as though he were packed in ice, his head bobbed and he retched again. When it was over, he leaned against the dirty sink, turned the faucet on, and cupping one hand under the stream brought the water to his mouth, then spit it out.

He made his way across the barroom to Susan.

"I think we better go back now."

She nodded.

Silently they walked out into a light rain.

Michael Marks waited for Joseph Eliav in the Upper Egyptian Gallery of the British Museum, a short walk from the Israeli agent's travel office in Russell Square. Eliav had requested a briefing before Barth left for the Soviet Union.

Moments later Eliav, medium-height and solid, in unusually good physical condition for a man in his mid-fifties, entered the gallery and approached the glass case enclosing a coffin from the First Dynasty.

"How is everything?" the Israeli asked.

"Fine. The boy's set to go out the end of the week. He'll be at the Metropole Hotel." They began to walk through the exhibit toward the wing housing Greek and Roman vases. "I think he was a good choice. Seems to know how to handle himself."

"And the girl?" Eliav asked.

Marks smiled. "She's really something—lots of energy, strong, but not overbearing. They should get along well. Barth will probably fall for her but even if he doesn't I'm sure he'll be glad she's there."

"I agree." They moved into the Second Vase Room, taking time to view Attic pottery from the fifth century B.C., with its scenes of gods and heroes.

"With any luck this one should go smoothly," Marks said. "Thanks for finding Barth for us."

Eliav nodded. "I'll tell the Colonel."

At the northwest staircase they parted company. Eliav took the stairs, Marks headed for the elevator in the adjacent First Egyptian Room. Riding down, he wondered why the Israelis wanted to send a girl along with Barth. The Russians actually wouldn't find his traveling alone suspicious. But Marks had worked with the Mossad chief in similar situations. He knew the Colonel well enough to know that he wouldn't be concerned about Barth's feeling lonely. No, there had to be more to sending the girl than that.

Six-Moscow

Steve stared out the window of the plane, thinking about his last hours in London. Mike had chopped his final security briefing to a flurry of compendious sentences followed by a curt: "Mind you, you can handle it. Just use your common sense." An extensive briefing was unnecessary. Steve could never prepare himself for all possible contingencies and trying courted the danger that too sharp a state of readiness would invite panic in the face of the unexpected. Elaborate training of an amateur also tended to undermine the advantages of innocence.

"When will we get to Moscow?" Susan, in the seat next to

him, was busy spreading Devon butter and strawberry jam over a dry scone.

"About three o'clock local time," he said, reaching for the book in the net pouch in front of him. He opened *The Hobbit* to the title page. "We should be in the hotel by six."

She nodded and shifted her legs. Steve peered out the window again. The British Airways plane banked left through a wisp of cloud and glided skyward, after some minutes leveling off at twenty-eight thousand feet.

Leaning back, he accidentally brushed against Susan's shoulder. She turned her eyes, a smile flicking the corners of her mouth. He reached for his book. He loved fantasies: knights and princesses, wizards and magic rings. His eyes devoured line after line, his forefinger poised to deliver the next page. It was only when he heard a rhythmic breathing and felt a head on his shoulder that he realized it had been some time since he'd absorbed a word of what he'd read.

About half a book later the plane dipped into a slow, gradual descent. Approaching the western edge of Moscow, Steve looked down at the forest of green sentinels broken by the sprawling dachas of the elite and the smaller izbas, squat peasant cabins. He kissed Susan's forehead lightly to wake her.

On the ground they checked through passport control with minimal delay. Luckily their names appeared on the list Sheremetyevo International Airport prints of all passengers due to arrive each day, a consistently less than accurate accounting. One half of the small two-page document given them by the Russian Embassy in London was torn off and retained by the stern-faced immigration officer. To Steve's surprise nothing was stamped in their passports. As they cleared the booth the immigration officer placed their visas in a special envelope. Within the hour it would be forwarded to the First Section, Seventh Department of the Second Chief Directorate—the KGB office that directed security with regard to American, British, and Canadian tourists.

Hundreds of people waited in line to check through the seven customs stations. Most were voyagers stranded from flights that had deposited them several hours earlier. Steve and Susan pulled their suitcases off the rotating conveyor belt and stood at the end of a long line whose male customs clerk looked much less intimidating than his female counterparts.

As three o'clock turned into four, then crawled toward five, the line moved gradually forward. Steve's impatience grew but Susan chatted casually in an effort to calm both of them. To their surprise most foreigners were cleared after only a cursory juggling of shirts and blouses, while the bags of Russian passengers disembarking from internal flights were subject to a stringent search. A short, wrinkled woman directly in front of them, dressed in a long black peasant dress with gold embroidery, appeared to have arrived from some Central Asian province. Her tattered cloth suitcase had been rifled, a tape measure produced, and every yard of material she harbored carefully measured—the results registered in a voluminous black book. As tears fell from her weary eyes, the customs agent held out his arm, palm up. Wiping her face with the back of a veined hand, the woman produced several worn bills and gave them to him.

Steve hoisted his and Susan's suitcases onto the check stand, wiping his moist palm against his pants. The Hebrew books they carried, totally unobtainable in the Soviet Union, were hidden in Susan's purse. Though Mike had assured them that Westerners' personal possessions and bodies were rarely searched upon entering Russia, a heaviness bore on Steve and his limbs felt weak. He tried to swallow but his mouth was too dry. Suddenly he felt fear: a nagging awareness that at any moment the secret police could burst through their wall of silence and grab them. What would follow was unknown, a terrifying hole in his experience that even his imagination could not fill.

Steve unlocked their suitcases and swung them toward the customs officer. The tall, pale man began probing through the various layers, randomly choosing a few articles to wrench free and shake into the air. Mike had made sure they packed no Western magazines containing the opulent advertising that contradicted Soviet descriptions of American life and consequently angered customs officials. In a back corner of Steve's bag the Russian found some Contac cold capsules. Carefully extending the bottle at arm's reach, he held it toward the window.

"Open," he ordered, thrusting the bottle at Steve.

"But they're only cold capsules."

"Open!"

Steve nodded nervously, unscrewed the cap, and shook a few of the capsules into his hand. The official took one, held it to the light, then returned it to him, ordering:

"Open!"

Steve, his sweaty fingers slipping on the smooth plastic, broke the outer shell of the capsule and dumped the red, yellow, and white granules into the customs agent's palm.

The Russian pushed the tiny balls over his skin with a forefinger, then dashed them to the ground.

"Passports," he demanded.

After a detailed inspection of the documents he slapped them on top of the suitcases, boomed "*horosho*," and shoved their bags to the far end of his long table.

"Come on, let's go to Moscow," Susan said excitedly, taking Steve's arm.

After a few minutes they located the Intourist desk and a driver who had been assigned to meet them at three. The elderly pockmarked man ushered them outside with a quick series of gestures; evidently he was as anxious to leave the airport as they were.

His boxlike black Zhiguli, a Soviet-made Fiat, was parked against the curb. He forced their luggage into the small trunk and they climbed into the back seat. Approaching the outskirts of the city, along the tree-lined Leningradskoye Highway, they passed the three stark tank traps that marked the spot where Russian troops turned back the Nazi advance. On both sides of the highway rows of prefabricated nine-, eleven-, and fourteen-story apartment houses blotted the gray sky. Their grand, numbing facades were cracked and peeling—victims of the instant aging inevitable when construction engineers are bent on throwing up the maximum square meters of floor space by a deadline in order to earn "Plan completed" bonuses.

The car turned into the wide, grass-lined Leningradsky Prospekt. Continuing into Gorky Street, the driver inched his way through traffic and trolleys and came to a halt on the eastern edge of Sverdlov Square, across from the towering Bolshoi Theater and in front of the Metropole Hotel. As they walked across the worn carpet at the entrance to the hotel, a song by the Beatles poured incongruously from the loudspeakers of the seventy-year-old edifice.

"Are you hungry, Susan?" Steve asked realizing they had not exchanged a word since customs.

"A little."

"Me too." He thought he should say something else, but didn't know what. She smiled warmly and took his arm.

After checking in they left their bags unopened on the large bed and hurried downstairs. Though Steve was anxious to make immediate contact with Zev Zaretsky and deliver the books, in order to behave like ordinary tourists they would have to dine in the hotel first. The prospect of lingering long in the restaurant made Steve restless. He'd been told that even the simplest meals in Moscow were rarely served in less than two hours.

In the dining room, Steve slipped the headwaiter a three-ruble note and asked that they be served as soon as possible. The headwaiter nodded and seated them at a crescent shaped leather banquette near a marble fountain, where they had a direct view of the dancers gliding around a pool of water. Mike had advised that Chicken Kiev, boneless breast of chicken filled with butter and fried in bread crumbs, was both palatable and generally available, unlike two-thirds of the items listed on the grease-spotted menu—so with Susan's approval Steve ordered it for two.

"I saw you at Mike's party the other night," Susan said. "I was going to introduce myself, but you seemed pretty out of it."

"Yeah, I guess I was, I don't remember much of what I did or who I spoke to at that party."

"I do."

For the second time since he met her, Steve felt disarmed. "What do you mean?"

"Well, you were dancing with one of my friends—Cindy. The

whole time she tried to talk to you, you kept looking around, not focusing on anything. You didn't even seem to hear the music. Later, Cindy said she couldn't figure out what she did wrong."

"Well, maybe she was trying too hard," Steve said, irritated that his indifference had been that obvious. "Why were you watching so closely?"

"Because you looked so cold and uninterested. I was intrigued."

Typical, Steve thought.

"I was wondering just how lonely you must be to make you act as if you didn't need anyone."

Steve felt a wave of resentment surface. Why couldn't she leave him alone? "What do you want?" he asked.

"Nothing." Her tone held warmth.

The food arrived. As Steve bent forward to lift a dripping piece of chicken to his mouth he caught sight of a man, sitting several tables away, eyeing Susan with apparently more than casual interest. Noticing Steve's gaze, the man diverted his attention to his food. Embarrassed, Steve quickly looked behind him at the huge stained glass wall, through which he could see the ghostlike silhouettes of people climbing and descending the hotel's main staircase.

Dmitri Karpov was angry that he had allowed the boy to spot him. Nervously, he fingered the pair of windshield wipers that lay on the tablecloth next to his plate. Like all Muscovite automobile owners, he removed his wipers; otherwise someone would have stolen them for resale on the black market. Soviet automobile factories, harassed into meeting production quotas, found little time to manufacture spare parts like windshield wipers.

Karpov cut into a strip of sturgeon, trying to figure out what it was about the girl that made him uneasy. She was attractive, but then he had known many attractive women—that wasn't it. Maybe it was her youth that set him on edge. He reached for his bottle of caraway-flavored Tminaya vodka and spilled a dash into his glass. They had no right to involve kids in this business. As the young couple headed for the exit, Karpov knocked down a shot of vodka and returned to his meal. There was no need to follow them—not yet.

Steve and Susan crossed the street and entered the fountained garden of Sverdlov Square, passing the bust of Karl Marx that sat on a massive granite base. Beyond the red medieval walls of Kitay-Gorod, the epicenter of town, rose the silver and gold belfries of the Zaikonopassky and Nikolsky monasteries. As most tourists do their first night in Moscow, they walked past the towering History Museum into Red Square. At the far end of the cobbled 440-yard plaza the turbulent beauty of St. Basil's Cathedral, with its onion-shaped spires, shone against the night. Nearer, in the center of the square at the base of the Kremlin's fortress walls, sat the low, somber, rectangular-shaped red granite mausoleum where Lenin's body was enshrined in an open casket.

"It's incredibly beautiful," Susan said, rushing across the cobbled pavement. "I can just see the Czar and Czarina parading through here in a gilded carriage drawn by chestnut stallions, the trumpets blaring, the crowd cheering. Can you imagine what it must have been like—the nobility dressed in flowing robes, dancing in large halls under sparkling chandeliers?" She stopped and stared past St. Basil's toward the Moskva River. "Have you ever read Tolstoy or Pasternak?"

"No, and I'm not much of a romantic either. Come on, let's go."

She looked at him, trying not to let her expression reveal her thoughts. She felt sorry for him. The hard line on his face was covering something, some pain she was determined to slip beneath.

Taking her arm, Steve moved through a group of people heading in the direction of October the 25th Street. The girls they passed wore drab dresses and sandals; the men, open-throated shirts, dark trousers, and sandals with socks.

"That must be GUM," Steve said, breaking the uncomfortable silence.

"Where?"

He pointed at a massive facade on the eastern edge of the square. "It's reputed to be the largest department store in the world, but I've been told it's really a series of separate shops under one roof."

"I want to look for a second," she said, hurrying toward the brightly lit store window. She seemed so untainted by cynicism, so free to embrace life, that Steve momentarily felt jealous. "Aren't you curious?" she asked and leaned the back of her head on his shoulder. "Let's go in tomorrow."

He moved away. "Maybe."

She turned, catching his eye. "It *is* kind of romantic being in Russia, isn't it?"

"Sure."

They crossed to a taxi stand opposite the square and found a waiting Volga M-124, a five-seater resembling a round Plymouth. Steve showed the driver the sheet of paper on which was written, in Russian, a street address in the mammoth Khoroshovo-Mnevniki housing compound. The driver nodded, threw the car in gear, and headed out Ulitza Dzerzhinsky toward the wide avenue that circles the central city. The streetlights cast an iridescent bluish glare across Moscow's ten-, twelve-, and fourteen-lane boulevards—memorials to Stalin, who chose to widen the already broad highways. Near the serpentine Moskva River they turned onto Zvenigorod Street, passing another of Stalin's testaments to excess, the Plamya building—a sister to the seven mock-gothic castles of sandstone, government structures whose spires, crowned by Red Stars, tower over the city. The taxi came to a halt in front of a mountain of prefabricated apartment blocks, numbing in size, pockmarked, naked—with no trees, shrubbery, or grass to break their monotony. Steve paid the fare and watched the Volga turn back toward the city. In London, Mike had told him that the taxi driver could be expected to call the KGB and report the address where he'd deposited two foreigners—which is why the address was not their real destination. From the Khoroshovo-Mnevniki compound it was a twenty-minute walk to the building on Ulitza Pekhotnaya where Zev Zaretsky lived.

As he and Susan crossed the dark, quiet entryway and entered the creaky double-door elevator leading to Zaretsky's apartment Steve hoped they hadn't been seen by the *dezhurnaya*, the building supervisor whose job, according to Mike, also included reporting the comings and goings of all strangers. He felt little excitement at the prospect of meeting a group of dissident Jewish activists; his greater concern was that they not be arrested for doing so.

Steve rapped on the door of apartment 802, and a large-eyed young man with curly hair, a bushy blond beard, wearing wrinkled jeans, pulled the door open. His nose was scarred and swollen and there were rope burns on his wrists.

"*Shalom*," he said, grabbing Steve's and Susan's hands with both of his.

Surprised that they were expected and startled by the warmth of Zaretsky's greeting, Steve managed a halting "*Sha-a-lom*." He often stuttered when he spoke Hebrew, particularly when he hadn't used the language for a while. In his childhood he had stuttered incessantly.

The apartment was small, colorless, and sparsely furnished. On a narrow bed which served in the daytime as a couch sat two men. They rose on seeing the Americans.

"I am Zev and these are my friends Andrei and Fayim," Zaretsky said in impressive Hebrew. "You are Steve and Susan?"

Steve nodded. Andrei, tall and childlike, approached with slow languid movements. Fayim, on the other hand, short, with restless eyes and a mop of stringy dark hair, rushed forward. Both appeared in their early twenties.

"Come, sit down," Zev suggested, leading Susan and Steve to a wood table surrounded by mismatched chairs.

"Let me help you," Fayim said, hurrying to pull out Susan's seat.

"What did he say?" she asked Steve, not understanding the rush of Hebrew.

"Nothing. He just offered to get your chair."

"Steve," she said, "I feel bad."

"Why?"

"They take such risks to learn Hebrew here and . . . well, I've never bothered with the language."

"Don't worry, Susan," he said, putting his hand on hers. "If it was illegal to learn Hebrew in the States I'm sure you'd be fluent by now."

She tried to smile.

Zev studied his guests. "We're very excited that you were able to come and . . ."

"Nothing happened at the airport?" Fayim interrupted anxiously. "The KGB didn't question you or confiscate anything?"

"No, we cleared customs without incident." He turned to Susan and said in English: "I think you'd better give them the books now."

She opened her purse, withdrew the volumes hidden there, and placed them on the table. A stiff silence hung in the room. Zev and Fayim reached for the printed pages simultaneously; Andrei, motionless, stared.

"Shamir's *King of Flesh and Blood*, Hertzberg's *Zionist Idea*, and Roth's *History of the Jews*," Fayim shouted. "All in Hebrew." He turned to Susan, forgetting she couldn't understand him. "You have no idea how important books like these are."

Zev held Hertzberg's classic tightly. "You must understand Soviet mentality to realize what these books mean to us. Everything here depends on the whim of the authorities. They expend so much energy on propaganda the result is an insatiable thirst for books. The uncensored sentence possesses an enormously exaggerated significance. Words transcend their ideas—they become symbols that nurture strength, fire the will to continue struggling. A book is something we can touch, hold on to when the road to freedom looks the darkest." Anger etched his words. "We can acquire nothing in Hebrew. In the stores Hebrew books are unavailable, in the libraries inaccessible without a security clearance. The situation is impossible. For a long time I studied a geology book. It was boring, I hated it; but it was in Hebrew so I read it over and over until I knew the meaning of every word."

"For some unknown reason the situation has suddenly worsened," Andrei said, slowly lighting a papirosi, a pungent cigarette with a hollow stem for a filter. "Several weeks ago the KGB managed to locate our advanced underground classes. In a coordinated sweep they confiscated our most important books. We have no idea how they discovered the locations of our classes, unless," he hesitated, "unless there are *seksoty*, secret police agents, among us."

"We need books to replenish our stock," Fayim added hurriedly, uncomfortable that Andrei had voiced their suspicion. Zev went into the kitchen, and Fayim changed the subject. "The three of us are Hebrew teachers. We offer classes any time that is convenient for our students."

"But what about your jobs?" Steve asked. "I was told that if a Soviet citizen is not employed he can be imprisoned as a parasite of the state. Don't you work?"

"Zev lost his position at the Lebedev Institute of Physics when he submitted his *kharakteristika*, a character reference form, to his superiors," Fayim explained. "The document must be filled out before one can apply for an Israeli visa. In order to avoid the charge that he should be prevented from leaving the country because he is privy to state secrets, he took a job as a maintenance man and teaches in the evenings. You saw the scars on his nose? Two months ago he was fired. Blacklisted and unable to find work, he was arrested by the KGB on the pretext of parasitism. Demanding the right to register as a private tutor, he went on a hunger strike. The KGB started force-feeding him every four days through his nostrils. He kept ripping out the tube. Finally they had to tie his hands down." Steve winced. "Like Zev, Andrei was fired and forced to find a job as a baker's loader. I am lucky enough to have a friend willing to falsely register me as his private secretary. I'm free the entire day but unfortunately must pay tax on income I never receive."

Susan leaned an elbow on the table and nudged Steve's hand. "What's he saying?"

Steve translated the conversation, then turned and met Andrei's eyes. "There's something I don't understand. You said books were confiscated, but what about your classes? Do the authorities allow you to teach them?"

"Several of us have been summoned and *requested* to refrain from conducting unauthorized classes In protest I applied to pay the tutor's tax, but instead of an account form received a letter stating that I could not give private lessons because there are no state programs for the study of Hebrew in the Soviet Union. I wrote back citing a program in Hebrew at the Institute of Eastern Languages at Moscow University—coincidentally closed to Jews—but I received no reply."

"That's only the beginning," Fayim said. "Zev and I were invited to a meeting with the assistant to the chairman of the Executive Committee of the City of Moscow, who informed us that our requests had been considered at the highest levels but rejected. We were told, 'It is not in the interest of the USSR that her citizens know Hebrew even if there was a desire among the Soviet people to learn the language, which there is not.'"

Steve had read enough to know that the Soviets were masters at keeping their multifarious population cowed. The randomness of the authorities' behavior, the fear fashioned from a continual waiting to confront the unexpected, numbed the people into passivity. Even the dissident Jews, the most successful of all Soviet underground groups, found their movement debilitated by

63

a policy of chaotic compromise and contradiction that simultaneously imprisoned certain activists, harassed and refused visas to others, while granting large numbers immediate emigration privileges.

Zev entered the room holding a tray bearing a bottle, several small glasses, brown bread, chunks of hard cheese, and green apples. As he set the food on the table Andrei reached for the clear bottle.

"I'm sorry we can't offer you any Stolichnaya, but since 1970 the best Russian brands are reserved for export." He poured out a round of drinks. "All we can get outside of the hard currency *Beryozka* shops is a harsh blend simply called vodka." Andrei smiled. "But after several glasses the taste is of minimal importance." He tossed back his head, brought the glass to his lips, and knocked down the contents in one quick gulp.

Steve followed suit. Coughing, he grabbed a heel of bread and forced it into his mouth, while his companions laughed.

"Next time you must finish it all at once," Andrei said.

Steve reached for more bread. "No problem."

"We were led to believe you would be going back to Israel after your visit here," Zev said.

"I guess so."

After a slight motion to Fayim, who rose quickly and moved toward the hall closet, Zev continued, "We would like to ask some advice and a favor."

Steve nodded. "Of course."

Fayim returned and dropped two books and an envelope in front of Zev. The top book was the blue, American paperback edition of Leon Uris's *Exodus*.

"Where did you get that?" Susan asked.

"Tourist," Zev answered, grasping the essence of her question, then he switched back to Hebrew. "It was brought to us several months ago. At the moment a team is working on translating the novel into Russian. We believe hand-circulated *samizdat* manuscripts will have the same staggering impact on Russia's Jews I'm told the book had on America's. But there is one aspect of the story that confuses us. We are considering changing it in our translation." He reached for a tumbler of vodka. "I thought while you are here I would ask your advice."

"Yes."

He tossed down the vodka effortlessly. "It deals with the love story. This relationship between Ari Ben-Canaan and the American Kitty." Zev hesitated, uncertain how to proceed. Finally he blurted out: "She's not Jewish. How could Leon Uris have done such a thing? How could he write a love story about the creation of the State of Israel and make the heroine Christian? We can't understand it."

Steve laughed at the unexpected turn in the conversation. "What's there to understand? A man was deeply touched by a woman. It's a special event, explored movingly in the book. Falling in love with someone of another religion is a problem and Uris probably wrote the story the way he did because that's the way relationships are—messy." For a moment Steve was aware of a former self taking over; he sounded like the Steve who lived before he killed Johnny Robinson.

"But we're afraid of the influence a literal translation might have," Fayim argued. "Jewish youth are already intermarrying at a high rate in Russia."

"As Jews are everywhere. It's the inevitable result of leaving the ghetto. Be concerned with the quality not the quantity of

Jewish life. Ari and Kitty won't encourage intermarriage; if anything, their anguish should give those in similar circumstances a moment of hesitation." Steve reached for the other book on the table. It was an aged, leather-bound volume, the edges of the spine worn away. Carefully Steve lifted the cover and turned several yellowed pages until he reached the frontispiece which told him it was a Hebrew Bible printed in Vilna in 1828.

"The book has been in my family for generations," Andrei said. "It's my only important possession."

Steve turned to the first words of Genesis, feeling the dryness of the pages as he lifted them between thumb and forefinger. The familiar Hebrew script leapt out at him. He'd enjoyed the Bible he'd learned as a child and the first sentence of the Five Books of Moses sang in his memory.

Closing the book, he waited for someone to speak. They would not have shown him the Bible unless they had a reason for doing so. The possibility that these young activists simply wanted to share the sight of a treasured possession with a Jewish visitor did not occur to him.

"Before emigrants leaving the Soviet Union can board the train for Vienna their bags are thoroughly searched," Zev began, breaking the stillness. "Any item can be confiscated under the pretext that it is historical property belonging to the state. The secret police spare no opportunity to harass departing Jews." He grabbed at his vodka. "Their only purpose is the pleasure of the sadist."

"We've had word that I will probably be getting my visa soon," Andrei said, pulling the heavy book near him. "I'm afraid the Bible will be taken when my bags are searched." His request, which was obvious now, was unspoken.

"Would you take the book to Israel?" Fayim blurted out, with the obsessive compulsion of those who fear if they don't perform an act personally it will never be accomplished. "If questioned at the border you could say the Bible's yours."

"But what if they open it and see the title page? They'll never believe I own a rare Hebrew book printed in Vilna in 1828."

Zev nodded at Andrei. Apparently they had considered the possibility. The tall Russian lifted the cover, fingered the leather, then turned to the page revealing the book's place of publication. "You're right, it would be unwise to let the KGB discover the Bible was printed here." With an even, graceful motion Andrei tore the page from the book. Setting the single sheet down, he closed the cover, and pushed the volume across the table. "That should minimize the danger."

"Could I have a pen and a piece of paper?" Steve asked Susan, noticing moisture glazed her eyes as she opened her purse. Though she didn't understand the conversation he realized she was following much of what was being said. He wrote his address on the sheet she gave him. "Here's where you can reach me in Jerusalem." He handed the paper to Andrei. "There's no phone, so you'll have to write or come by."

"Thank you," Andrei said, folding the address into his shirt pocket.

"If we're not imposing on you there's another favor I'd like to ask," Zev said. He again poured a large quantity of vodka for himself and spilled some into Steve's three-quarters full jigger. The liquid overflowed onto the table. "My brother's in Israel and from what I've been able to piece together it seems he hasn't received a letter from me for over four months." Zev paid no attention to the spilled vodka. Instead he reached for the unaddressed envelope Fayim had brought from the closet. "I was hoping that you would take this to him. It contains personal news about my wife and child."

Steve took the letter. "I guess I could find a safe place to hide it."

"I appreciate your help more than you realize." His smile faded. "I've had no contact with my brother since he left Russia. Nothing. All I know is that he's in the immigrant absorption center in Mevasseret Zion, outside Jerusalem." Zev gulped the vodka, then roughly dropped the empty glass on the table. "My brother's name is Yevgeny Zaretsky. You shouldn't have any trouble finding him."

Steve nodded. "I'll give him the letter personally."

Fayim, who had been picking disinterestedly at some hard cheese, pushed the chunk to the end of the table, out of reach. "You must understand our existence here," he said. "When we apply for visas we become lepers. Anyone who associates with us is assumed to have contracted our disease. To protect our friends we must not see them, ever. We're forced to live on a tiny island, confined with other lepers." He tugged on the back of his neck, then let his hand fall forward. The room held the silence.

Sensing the flow of conversation had broken, Susan touched the edge of Steve's hand, and pointed to his watch crystal. It was almost eleven. Mike had warned them that Moscow's cultural activities and cafés closed early. To avoid suspicion, they should be back in the hotel by midnight.

Steve took a last sip of vodka and nudged the Bible and letter toward Susan, who put them in her purse. He rose from the table. "I'm afraid it's late."

Zev bounced to his feet, his pale face flushed by the vodka. "You are right. It will take us some time to accompany you to the hotel."

"Will we see you again?" Fayim asked hopefully.

"I don't know. I can't see any reason why not."

"It would probably be safest if you purchased tickets in the hotel and attended the ballet tomorrow night," Andrei said. "But we'd consider it an honor if you would join us for dinner here the following evening. Many of those who've been refused visas want to meet you. They're very anxious to talk about Israel."

Steve nodded.

"Could you arrive at seven o'clock?" Zev asked. "That would give us more time together."

"Sure."

They insisted on accompanying the Americans to the vicinity of the Metropole hotel, and led Steve and Susan to the escalator descending into the Moscow subway. They glided almost noiselessly from station to station, the Russians, intrepidly garrulous, firing a battery of personal questions at Steve and Susan that culminated in a short but raucous lesson on Arabic curses from Steve, who felt their Hebrew was all too Biblical. At Prospekt Marx they piled onto the platform.

It was dangerous for the Russians to be seen near the meticulously watched Intourist Hotels, so Zev accompanied Steve and Susan to the street, alone. On entering Sverdlov Square, Steve stopped.

"You'd better not go any further," he cautioned. "We can find our way from here."

Reluctantly Zev agreed. "All right." He grabbed Steve's

hand, locking it between his palms, then leaned over and planted a wet kiss on Susan's cheek. "Thank you, both of you." A moment later he was gone.

Susan and Steve entered the quiet lobby and took the elevator to the third floor. The white-coated woman stationed behind the spacious desk at the entrance to the hallway, as her counterparts were on every floor of the hotel, handed Steve the key to their room. As he slipped it into the lock of room 315 and pushed his way inside she lifted the receiver on her telephone and began to dial.

"What were you talking to them about?" Susan asked, sitting on the edge of the bed and letting her shoes fall to the floor.

Steve pointed to the ceiling, signifying the room was probably bugged. She nodded, crossed to the dresser, and began to rummage through her overnight case. After several long minutes she turned toward him, her hands empty. "I can't find my shampoo." No frustration marred her voice. "I'm always losing things. I really don't know why."

"Would you like to use some of mine?"

"If you have enough."

He went to his suitcase and removed the unbreakable tube of shampoo he'd placed in the side pouch, for some reason pleased with the prospect of giving it to her. He tossed the shampoo across the room and she caught it, one-handed. As she closed the bathroom door behind her he opened her purse, removed Zev's letter, and put it in his back pants pocket. Then he took out the Bible, studied the embossed title for a moment, and placed it in his suitcase between a stack of shirts. If for any reason they were searched he wanted all incriminating evidence to be in his possession.

After a while Susan emerged, clad in a yellow plaid robe, drying her hair on a hotel towel.

"Do you want me to close the window until your hair dries?" he asked.

"No, that's not necessary," she said. She lay down on the bed with her back toward him, reached up, and turned on the nightstand lamp.

"Should I shut off the overhead light?"

"If you want."

She tossed her robe on a chair and slipped under the covers. Steve snapped the light off, leaving the room illuminated by the small lamp at her side, its rays stretching part way across the bed. Her face lay at the edge of the brightness, half in shadow. As he neared she rolled onto her side and studied his face.

Steve removed his outer garments, quickly pulled off his underwear, and crawled in beside her. He wanted to say something noncommittal, could think of nothing, so he remained silent. Though she was attractive and had a good body he didn't feel like starting the game. What was the point? But if he did try, he wondered—would she be willing? On the other hand, if he didn't make a move she might be disappointed, might think he considered her unattractive. Possibly she was into sex and was waiting for him to do something?

Diverting her eyes, Susan pushed deeper into the pillow.

Steve watched the shadows move across her face as she shifted position. I can see right through her confused look, he thought. She really doesn't want me to come on to her but she is thinking she should be pleasant, that she should be careful not to put any more pressure on me. She thinks I'm cynical and bitter and probably won't admit to herself that that makes me more attractive. She's probably feeling pretty frustrated. I haven't shown much interest in her and here I am less than a foot away and doing nothing.

He turned onto his back. Actually he felt ridiculous lying in bed with this girl, neither of them talking or willing to move. He propped his head on his elbow. "Susan, are you comfortable? Do you think you'll be able to sleep?"

"Yes," she said, sitting up. "But I'm afraid I'm going to have nightmares of you slowly driving me crazy with politeness. Cut it out. It's such a dishonest form of indifference."

He failed to suppress a smile. "Who said I was indifferent?" He inched closer. "That's absurd." He kissed her.

She moved her lips against his. "Steve," she said, "I'd love to sleep with you if you're really *feeling* something."

In similar situations, knowing he felt nothing, Steve had always lied. But now his emotions resisted control. "In that case we'd better forget it," he said, pulling away. "We have a job to do and we both have a lot of things on our minds. It would be best if we just . . ."

"Of course," Susan said. The tone in her voice was casual, unconcerned. It hurt him.

Reaching over her, he turned out the lamp. In the darkness he watched patterns of light move past the hotel window. He considered putting his underwear back on but decided it would be too much trouble.

Seven-Moscow

Steve awoke to the stillness of the first hour of dawn. He'd slept poorly with dreams that came and went like tides in his mind. The sun, slanting through the window, threw a patch of light on the white plaster wall opposite the bed. Soon the rays of brightness widened and began to touch their bodies with gentle warmth. He rested on his side against the pillow and she on her back half turned toward him, her mouth parted slightly, her firm small breasts rhythmically rising and falling with each breath. He reached out to touch her and then stopped. Turning, he inched his way off the bed and walked into the bathroom, still half asleep.

His feet felt cold on the tile floor. He closed the door behind him, stared at the tub for a moment, then turned on the hot water. Soon mist filled the small chamber, clouding the mirror. When he was a kid, fat and embarrassed, Steve used to stretch across a steaming tub each morning before his parents woke, hoping the heat would melt away some of his blubber. Now, almost too slim, he leaned his face into the vapor and inhaled through his mouth and nostrils. His meeting with Zev, Andrei, and Fayim played over and over in his mind, their faces dancing in the mist. The pain they suffered became his.

After a while Steve's head cleared. He turned on the cold faucet, waited a few minutes, then stepped into the water.

Susan took a long time to get dressed, which made him restless. Seated on the edge of the bed, she slipped on her clothes in a slow series of motions far more seductive than her naked body.

After breakfast they embarked on a prescheduled Moscow city tour with a group of about twenty other English-speaking sightseers. They wandered through the Kremlin into the former residence of the royal family, now a formidable museum. As they approached the three churches within the Kremlin walls, someone asked their Intourist guide about religion in the USSR. "There are people who believe in God," the guide answered mechanically. "For them there are no restrictions, but being a Communist and believing in God are contradictory." Back in the bus she spoke of the great cultural advances Russia had made since the 1917 Revolution. From the Kremlin they drove to the permanent National Economic Achievements Exhibition on Mira Prospekt, watched over by a towering silvery monument to the Soviet cosmonauts. Engraved into the base of the triangular-shaped structure, stretching his arm triumphantly behind the space heroes, was Vladimir Ilyich Lenin, the ubiquitous icon. Everywhere inside the seventy-pavilion exhibit, as everywhere inside the Soviet Union, the guardians of history had erected secular shrines: statues, busts, and paintings of Vladimir Ilyich guiding, admonishing, gesturing, or striding boldly into the bright future. Perpetuating the illusion of immortality projected a screen behind which each successive generation of leaders could hide.

The bus deposited Steve and Susan at the edge of Sverdlov Square opposite the columned facade of the Bolshoi Theater. A large crowd had gathered in front of the Metropole, spilling into the street. The object of its attention was a blue Chevrolet Impala. Steve threaded between the people, Susan lagging a step behind. Effortlessly, a solid, powerfully built man cut through the crowd toward Susan. As he passed behind her, he moved his lips close to her ear and whispered in heavily accented English: "Meet me at three in Hermitage Park. Alone." He melted into the milling people without breaking stride. Susan tried to catch a glimpse of him but he had disappeared. His voice had sounded familiar. She wondered who he was, what he wanted, where she had heard that voice before. She realized she wouldn't find out unless she followed his instructions.

Emerging from the edge of the crowd, Dmitri Karpov circled toward the street. When he reached the blue Impala he slipped in front of a matronly woman staring through the window at the upholstery, and unlocked the door. Inside the car he was struck by the same feeling he had had the previous night watching Susan at dinner. She was much too young to be caught in the web of an invisible war.

As Steve and Susan entered the hotel dining room, several

waiters moved toward them anxious for the *treshkas*, three-ruble notes, Steve was using to carve a path through supposedly tipless Soviet Russia. They lunched on dry sturgeon and watery stroganoff. Inefficiency could be deferred by bribery, but insufficiency remained insurmountable.

"Shall we go up to the room and rest for a while?" Susan suggested as they moved into the lobby.

"All right."

In their room she moved immediately into the bathroom. As the door closed behind her Steve dropped onto the side of the bed and kicked off his shoes. Tiredness seemed to explode inside him, a tiredness born of much more than the morning's excursion. He closed his eyes, shifted restlessly, and tried to free his mind of all thoughts.

Sometime later Susan emerged dressed in her robe. She crossed the room, her feet slapping softly on the floor, and sat on the bed. He opened his eyes.

"Hi," she said quietly.

Steve smiled.

A long silence filled the room, broken only by the sound of traffic in the street below.

"I was wondering," she said after a while. "Have you been hurt badly . . . by a woman?"

He sat up. "Yes."

"Would you tell me about it?"

"What for?"

"I'd like to hear."

"If you really want to." He shrugged. "It started when I was seventeen. I went out with this girl for three years. I gave everything I could to her, my experiences weren't complete unless we shared them. She graduated high school the semester after me and came up to Berkeley. I'd already been there half a year. I had played around with a lot of girls in the dorms and stupidly thought I'd done what there was to do. When she arrived I was ready to settle down. But the boys in her living unit were not very obliging.

"One rainy afternoon I popped over for a visit without phoning first. I found her and her roommate having a picnic lunch in their room with two guys. I excused myself, plowed down the stairs three at a time, and burst out of the stairwell crying—more shocked at the intensity of my reaction than at finding her with somebody else. She started going out with Alan, the guy from the picnic. I was beside myself with jealousy. I couldn't bear the thought that she was doing the same things with him one night that she was doing with me the next. The pain was excruciating, I couldn't get any work done. In the end we had a tremendous fight. I don't even remember what it was about. I think I was trying to force her to go out with me by threatening physical violence to myself. After this horrid scene in my room she went home. I called to apologize, but she couldn't talk. She was crying hysterically. I begged her to let me come over for a few minutes so I could apologize, but she said no. I threw the phone against the wall, shattering it. Then, I ran to her dorm.

"Outside, below her room, I gathered a few stones to toss at her window, but before I could throw any, she heard me call. Not knowing what to do with the rocks, I put them in my pocket." Steve exhaled heavily. "She screamed that I should go away, that she was scared of me. Heads began to pop out of windows. I begged her to come down just for a few seconds. I had picked some wildflowers I wanted to give her. I began to yell something when my voice was drowned by a siren. From a lower balcony I heard some girls say something about the housemothers calling the police. Next thing I knew I was running down the street, shaking inside, petrified that the police would find the rocks in my pocket, yet unable to slow down and throw them away."

Steve had been gazing at the floor. When he finished he raised his head and felt her eyes on him. The glassiness in her gaze told him that she had suffered as much through the telling as he. Neither of them said anything.

He was about to rise, anxious to seek sanctuary in the bathroom, when she began to speak. "I was at Radcliffe for a year before I moved to England. I mentioned I had a boyfriend at Harvard, Paul Schiffer. At one time I loved him deeply, committedly, but he broke that commitment by neglect, by devoting his entire energies to ambition, to maintaining a status he had never really achieved. It took me months to admit to myself that I no longer loved him. It was the first time for so many things, and it's difficult to let go even when there's nothing left to hold. I know eventually I'll feel deeply about someone else but I will never be the same—it was the first time." Sitting back on the bed, she lifted her knees to her chin, exposing bare thighs. "He never would have finished the school year without me. We took some of the same classes. He rarely went to his and I had to do all the work for the ones we had together. He convinced our sociology professor to let us do our research paper as a team. He was so busy by the winter with his organizations and speeches, people in the house where we lived had to make an appointment to see him. Finally when nothing was getting accomplished on our Race and Ethnic Relations paper I made a specific appointment to sit down and discuss what we were going to do. He didn't show up. He had a legitimate excuse, but ultimately it was still an excuse. In the end I wrote it myself and signed both our names. During semester break this guy Ron came up from New York and took me out a few times. Paul fell apart. He started crying, pleading with me to believe he was sorry, that he'd be more considerate. He was afraid I'd walk out on him. He begged me not to go out with Ron again, so I didn't. I think Paul considered it some sort of triumph. Later I found out he'd been screwing this girl in the dorms for months."

Steve stretched onto the bed and inched close to her. The act of confession had knitted a fragile bond between them. He felt a tenderness for her he would not allow himself to admit.

Suddenly he reached up and pulled her against him. The ends of her hair brushed against his face. They kissed, slowly exploring each other's mouths. She touched her tongue to his ear. "If you tell me you're not feeling anything I'm going to kick you where it hurts. Then you'll have a real excuse."

Steve laughed. He pulled off his clothes and untied her robe. "Are you protected?" he asked.

"Yes."

He hadn't asked that question in a long time. He ran his hands over her breasts, touching the gold name necklace she wore, feeling a sudden desire to tell her he cared. Instead he moved across her leg, wondering in some back part of his mind if he was beginning too quickly, if there shouldn't be more foreplay. He probed for the pathway into her, pushed forward, met an instant of resistance, then . . . Starting to move, he felt a warm hand on his buttocks. "Stay still," she said. Puzzled, he obeyed. In a pinch of pleasure, he felt her vaginal walls contracting against his penis. She held there for a minute, then relaxed some hidden muscles and waited. Slowly tightening against him again she felt a surge roll through his stationary body. She remained there longer this time before gradually dropping away. As she closed around him a third time he emitted a muffled grunt, wanting desperately to move and achieve ejaculation and stay still and prolong the pleasure. She strained, pressing harder. And he came.

The pulsating of his penis subsided. He lay on one shoulder still inside her, half hard. She shifted to the side and he slipped out, the odor of sex mingling with the other scents of their bodies.

He played with the ends of her hair, letting them cover his fingers. "Where did you learn to do that?"

"I read about it in a book," she said, smiling.

He thought uneasily that she was too experienced for her age. It was almost as if she'd been trained.

A soft silence settled over the room. After a short while Susan made her breathing regular and slow, imitating the initial stages of sleep. Minutes passed. Soon Steve rose, pulled on his clothes, scribbled her a note saying he was going for a walk, and left the room. She waited long enough to be certain he wasn't coming back for something he forgot, and dressed quickly. She had counted on him being unable to stay still for more than a few minutes. Checking her watch, she saw that she would have no trouble reaching Hermitage Park on time. If Steve came back to the room before she returned she could always explain that she woke, found him gone, and went for a walk herself.

As Steve hurried through Red Square the attention of every Russian seemed to linger on him. His patchwork shirt and corduroy Levi's were a glaring contrast to the gray mass that flowed around him. Many dark eyes fixed on his worn leather boots. The quality of Russian consumer products, especially shoes, was remarkably low. A sign on a pair of shoes in the GUM window read 50 rubles. On an average salary of 140 rubles per month, that was an impossible expense.

Just as Steve was about to enter the department store he felt a hand on his shoulder. A couple, who appeared to be his age, stood awkwardly opposite him.

"We saw you Red Square," the male said in halting English, pointing behind him. "You American?"

"Yes."

He grinned, saying something to his companion in Russian. Then turning to Steve he said, "I Pyotr. This is my girl Anna." She smiled, embarrassed as he grabbed her stiffly around the waist.

"I'm Steve."

"Maybe if you not busy you come with us," Pyotr gesticulated, urging him back toward Red Square. "We not see many little Americans."

Steve laughed at the misused word. "Okay."

They led him past the patient line of sightseers waiting for a glimpse of Lenin's casket. Near the Rossiya Hotel they turned toward the grassy bank of the Moskva River. Settling down away from anyone who might overhear their conversation, Pyotr picked nervously at the grass. "It good in America?" he asked eagerly.

"There are a lot of things that are wrong but yes, it's good in America."

"Where are you from?"

"California."

"Ah." He smiled. "Cowboys."

"Yeah, and Indians," Steve said.

"Is it expensive to live in America?"

"It's getting worse all the time."

"Here good things cost much," he stated, extending his hands in exasperation. "I want buy transistor radio. For me it cost fifty rubles. In tourist shop twenty dollars. I need only more five dollars. Maybe you help me?" His funereal expression, if calculated to evoke compassion, was almost succeeding. Steve remained silent, reluctant to respond. "Please, I give ten rubles for five dollars."

"I can't," Steve said, his voice bordering on harshness.

Pyotr transmitted his decision to Anna, who responded with a flurry of Russian. "Steve, maybe in room, American newspapers and magazines."

"I'm sorry. I didn't bring any with me."

"Records. Simon and Garfunkel, Led Zeppelin, Credence Clearwater, Willie and the Poor Boys—you have in hotel?" Pyotr asked, strained hope in his voice.

"I'm afraid not. But how did you know about Willie and the Poor Boys? Can you get American albums here?"

"No. We get nothing. I have a friend, Cleveland, Ohio. He sends records." The girl whispered something in Russian.

"Steve, do you have a car?"

"Yes," he said, not sure if it would have been kinder to lie.

"Then for you five dollars is little. I give fifteen rubles. Please."

"No," Steve said angrily. "I can't take the risk."

Again Anna whispered something to her boyfriend. This time Pyotr rose. "Excuse me, we must go meet friends."

Steve laughed to himself. He was sure they'd find their five dollars. As they disappeared into Red Square, suddenly lonely, Steve decided to return to the hotel and see if Susan was awake.

* * *

From Sverdlov Square Susan entered Petrovka Street and melted into the crowd on the busy shopping boulevard. When she reached Sadovaya Street, the belt of grass and trees that circles the inner city, Susan stopped. On the edge of the sidewalk before the intersection stood a long, saffron-colored tank: a kvas truck. A white-coated woman was serving glass mugs of the fermented peasant drink to the row of patrons, many of whom were reading newspapers as they waited. Though she wasn't thirsty, Susan joined the line. Soon she received a glass of kvas. The thick liquid, made from water dripped through burnt bread, tasted malty and bitter. Susan sipped the drink slowly—she was still a little early. When only the coffeelike grounds at the bottom were left she returned the mug to the woman, who tossed the muddy residue onto the ground and submerged the glass under water.

At the huge zebra-striped intersection, Petrovka Street turned into Karietny Riad, or Carriage Street, named for the number of coachworks once located there. To the left lay Hermitage Park, a popular rendezvous point always swollen with Muscovites on hot summer evenings. Small, with ponds, statues, and leafy trees, it contained several wooden theaters, the site of plays by writers that suit the restraints of socialist realism—Gorki, Chekhov, Mayakovsky, Bulgakov.

The man in front of the Metropole had not mentioned a specified meeting place so Susan decided to stroll along the paths until contacted. As she stepped off the curb a small black Zaporozhets-968 pulled out of traffic and skidded to a halt in front of her. A door opened and after a moment's hesitation, she got in. Dmitri Karpov rejoined the flow of vehicles. With his left hand he fingered the cigarette lighter inside his jacket pocket.

* * *

Dejected, Pyotr lagged behind Anna as they walked past the forboding statue of Felix Dzerzhinsky rising from the middle of the square bearing his name. For a moment he stared at the great windows of the building, most with heavy curtains drawn across them to prevent laser monitoring of the plate-glass vibrations, then he hurried after Anna into the Center. At Alexandr Zavorin's First Directorate offices she left him and took the stairs down to the wing occupied by the First Section, Seventh Department of the Second Chief Directorate. One of the hundred staff officers responsible for controlling tourists inside the Soviet Union, Anna would need to pull Pyotr's file from those of the other 1,600 agents and part-time informants the Seventh Department used.

Pyotr fidgeted nervously in the wooden chair, waiting to be summoned. The harsh glare of the globes overhead penetrated his skull and settled into a headache that pressed out from the back of his eyes. His mouth was dry. Having failed on his first major assignment, he expected retribution to be severe. Finally over an hour later he was led into the sumptuous office.

"Please sit down," Zavorin said, pointing to the low chair opposite the desk. "Would you like some tea?"

"No, thank you," Pyotr said, though he was thirsty. Zavorin turned toward the silver samovar resting on the table near the wall and drew himself a cup of rich mahogany-colored tea, sweetening it with three spoonfuls of sugar. His thoughts elsewhere, he stirred the liquid for a long time. One of his surveillance teams had just reported that they had lost the girl. She'd entered a black Zaporozhets-968, disappearing in traffic before she could be followed. Zavorin removed his spoon and set it on a napkin. The surveillance unit had, however, obtained the car's license number; it would be located shortly.

"You made contact with the American?" Zavorin asked, returning to Pyotr.

The boy nodded.

Zavorin spilled some tea into the saucer, and lifting the saucer in both hands, drank the hot liquid. "And?" he said.

"I'm sorry." Pyotr wanted to escape, but Zavorin's gaze riveted him in place. "I talked with the American. We sat on the grass near the Moskva River." He spoke quickly. "But I could not induce him to exchange money. He wasn't interested. He couldn't be persuaded. Anna said that he probably . . ."

"Had been instructed to avoid all encounters with the black market," Zavorin finished his sentence for him.

"Yes," the boy said with relief, the burden of his failure partially lifted.

"Yet if you approached him in the proper manner, evoking a delicate balance between sympathy and the contempt for the ruling class Barth's background betrays, he should have been susceptible."

"But I . . ."

"No matter," Zavorin interrupted with a wave of his hand. "It would have been advantageous to have the charge of currency speculation to hold over the boy's head but such evidence is not crucial. At the moment Barth is walking straight down the path we carved for him. Operation Cloverleaf is proceeding as planned." Zavorin stopped and sipped from his saucer. In the excitement over his success he was talking too much. No one must suspect that Steve Barth's trip to Russia was a Soviet-planned operation, that they needed an American sent to Moscow who'd return to Israel and activate the Soviet sleepers there, without the boy or anybody else realizing it. Zavorin took particular delight in the fact that the KGB had maneuvered the Israeli Colonel into recruiting Barth for them.

He took a file folder from the edge of his desk, opened it, and began reading. "Now, young man, if you will excuse me."

"Yes, Comrade General." Pyotr bolted to his feet and hurried out of the room.

Without looking up Zavorin grunted disdainfully and turned over a page in the file: a dossier of the CIA case officer, Phillip Fleske. Soon his mind left the printed text. He thought about the Americans, how naive they were, how little they understood the KGB, even after all their studies and books. The CIA was an intelligence service, limited by America's civilization; the KGB, an unrestrained army, trained on a mass scale, drawing on national compulsory service. Democratic man did not comprehend that the KGB operated like a factory. Although he was not staggered by the fact that General Motors produced four thousand cars every twenty-four hours, he was shocked by the news that the KGB planted three hundred spies in the foreign world daily. Russia understood and exploited this weakness. America's espionage system was effective only in open battle, when her mental factories were forced to retool. Russia would never go to war with the United States; she could accomplish her aims in peacetime.

A knock on the door broke Zavorin's train of thought. His private secretary, Yuri Pirozhkov, a tall balding officer with a drooping moustache, entered the room. He held a red-tipped classified memorandum, which he gave to the Major General, then stood to the side, silent.

"What!" Zavorin shouted, slamming his hand on the table. "Who the hell . . ." His pale face flushed, he glared at his secretary. "Get Grigorenko up here! Immediately! And ready a detachment of police."

The balding Pirozhkov ran from the room and grabbed the phone on his desk. He'd never seen his boss quite so upset.

Steve quietly pushed the hotel door open, not wanting to wake Susan. Inside, to his surprise, he found the room empty. Most likely she hadn't slept long, had gone for a short walk, and would be back soon. If he went out they'd probably miss each other again. In his suitcase he found a paperback edition of novelized *Star Trek* scripts and dropped into a chair near the window.

The descending sun cast an orange sheet across Steve's face, the soft light warming his cheeks. Soon the disc dipped below the horizon, the underside of the clouds soaking up the last traces of color. Steve tossed his book on the floor, not bothering to mark the place, and stared out at the array of massive structures comprising Moscow's skyline. As the minutes dragged by, seeming to stick to each other, he began to worry about Susan. He couldn't imagine where she could be. Finally unable to sit any longer he went downstairs.

The aging lobby was quiet. Most guests were in their rooms resting before dinner. At the small kiosk across from the front desk he bought postcards to send to his parents and Mike. Inquiring how much stamps to the United States and England cost, he was informed curtly that mail rates are the same to all capitalist countries. He scribbled short notes on both cards, then wandered outside. The night was warm and comfortable, the streetlights spreading a bluish haze over the sidewalk. To his right the Bolshoi, fiercely illuminated, dominated the square.

There was no sign of Susan. Steve paced the length of the street, keeping the Metropole entrance in sight. The fear that something might have happened to her crept into conscious thought, but he pushed the possibility away. She was fine. She'd probably stumbled onto something interesting and was pursuing it. She'd be back soon.

His legs grew tired. Suddenly he wondered if he had missed her, if she'd entered the hotel while he wasn't looking. He ran down the street, rushed through the lobby, and took the stairs three at a time. Bursting into the room, he called her name. She wasn't there. He stood still, breathing heavily, sweat coating his face, the knot in his stomach hardening.

He closed the door behind him. Abruptly it struck him that this was no game, no simple diversion from the tediousness of his life. He was in a country where the authorities know no restraints, where the slightest mistake, the most minutely misspoken word could bring the secret police crashing down on him. What would follow was inevitable: interrogation, beatings, imprisonment. And Susan, if anything happened to her. . . . He shook involuntarily.

A tapping on the door fractured his thoughts. It was Susan. It had to be. He ran across the room and flung the door open. "Susan, I . . ."

Three men entered wearing the blue shoulder boards and collar tabs of uniformed KGB police units. One grabbed Steve's arm, twisted it behind his back, and held him against the wall. The other two began searching the room.

"What are you doing?" Steve shouted, surprise momentarily anesthetizing the fear inside him.

The man clutching his wrist squeezed it tighter. "You're under arrest," he hissed.

Steve went limp.

Eight-Moscow

The burly officer shoved Steve down some stairs and through a door he had opened by pressing a button. They entered an older section of KGB headquarters, and headed up a flight of stairs, these with wire screens, floor to ceiling, to prevent anyone from leaping over the railing. Pushing through another door, this one requiring several buttons to be pressed in a coded sequence, they entered a long, damp corridor. The officer led Steve into the last of a row of interrogation rooms.

The stark rectangular chamber had chairs lined against each of the four walls. The ceiling was patched with loose acoustical

tile. In the center of the room Colonel Petr Grigorenko sat behind
a desk attached to a long table in a T-formation. As they entered he
barked something in Russian and the guard forcibly seated Steve
against the wall.

There were no windows. The stagnant air was edged by the
odor of the guard's unwashed uniform. Steve's heart beat wildly,
he felt each irregular breath pulled into his lungs. The seconds
dragged. No one spoke. The silence pressed against his ears.

A plainclothesman strode into the room carrying a worn
leather briefcase and sat at the table. He was middle-aged, barrel-
chested with white balding hair. He reminded Steve of David in
London. He wore the same masking smile.

"Please sit at the table," the man said, indicating the seat
directly across from him.

Steve complied immediately, surprised at the absence of
accent in the Russian's English. It sounded American.

"I am Nikolai Prestin. Your name please," he requested.

"Steven Barth."

"Passport?"

"It's in the hotel."

The man nodded, lifted the flap on his briefcase, then
stopped. "I understand you've been rather busy since you arrived
in the Soviet Union. Went to a little party last night, didn't you?"

"I don't know why you brought me here," Steve said. "What
have I done wrong?"

The Russian pulled a fresh file from his briefcase and began to
leaf through the pages.

"Is it illegal to talk to Soviet citizens?" Steve pressed him
nervously.

"No, but it *is* illegal to consort with known hooligans."

"Hooligans! Who said the people I was with are hooligans? They are just young people interested in talking to someone from the West, so they invited me to their apartment, that's all."

Prestin looked thoughtful. "It is my understanding that in the United States ignorance of a law or of committing a crime is not an acceptable excuse. I am afraid you erred in your judgment."

"I want to speak to the American ambassador," Steve said.

"I'm sorry, but at such a late hour that is not possible."

"All right, then if I'm under arrest, I demand to be charged and told specifically which law I have violated."

"Shut up!" Prestin shouted. "You make no demands here!"

His words struck Steve like a sledgehammer.

The interrogator lit a cigarette. "I'm afraid you're in very serious trouble. It will go better for you if you cooperate, otherwise . . ." He sucked on the cigarette, allowing the implication to go unspoken. "When were you last in Israel?" the Russian asked quickly.

"I've never been to Israel."

"Who sent you to Moscow?"

"Nobody sent me."

"What was your purpose in coming here?"

"None. I'm a tourist."

"What kind of messages were you carrying for the Jews?"

"None. I told you, I'm on vacation."

"Why did you choose Moscow?"

"Why not, it's a nice city, isn't it? You live here."

Nikolai Petrovich Prestin strummed his fingers on the desk "I have plenty of time. We will remain here until you decide to answer truthfully."

"As far as I'm concerned we can sit in this room forever, you'll die long before I will."

No facial reaction. "You have been associating with known hooligans," Prestin said. "When were you last in Israel?"

"I told you," Steve said angrily, "I've never been to Israel."

"Why were you traveling with a CIA agent?"

Shock sucked the breath from Steve. He reached for the handkerchief on the table, his hand shaking.

The interrogator moved close and leaned over menacingly. "A CIA agent. Why were you traveling with a spy?"

"What . . . what are you talking about?"

"Susan Stern works for the CIA. Come on. You know that."

"No. It's not true." He dropped against the back of the chair, hands clenched together around the damp handkerchief.

"Look, son, you're in a lot of trouble. I want to help you, but I can't unless you cooperate. We know you spent the last year in Jerusalem, that you were flown to London and assigned to Susan. Now what was her mission in Moscow?"

"How can I tell you . . ."

"We know the two of you contacted Zev Zaretsky and the other Zionists."

The color was gone from Steve's face. He said nothing.

"You can't deny it. That was only a cover. Susan's mission in Moscow. Come on."

Steve stared at his hands. The globe overhead was too bright; the tiredness was tugging at him, swallowing him.

"Susan Stern—they wanted you to go to Russia together."

His head came up slowly, his eyes reaching the policeman's, inches away from him. They were small and hard. The interrogator kept talking. He sensed he was on the verge of victory.

The kid was an amateur, untrained. He had little resistance left. One more shove and everything would come out.

"You agreed to accompany Susan to Russia, right? They gave you some books to bring to Zaretsky. Books desperately needed by the Hebrew teachers. They told you what you were doing was important. They introduced you to a young girl your age. Maybe they even made it look like you were in charge, implied that they only sent her as a traveling companion so you'd appear less suspicious. Take your time. Is that how it happened?"

"Yes." His lips hardly moving, the word escaped his mouth just above a whisper. Grigorenko could not hear the answer, it was too quietly spoken. He read it instead from Barth's face.

"Repeat it," the interrogator said. Push it into him. Make the boy hear himself squirming, betraying. That keeps the confession flowing. Once they start, keep them moving.

"Yes."

Some of the hostility dropped from the interrogator's face. He moved aside and stood out of the glare of the globe. "They didn't tell you she was a CIA agent, did they?"

Steve shook his head. It felt heavy, hard to move.

"They didn't tell you what they were up to. Didn't want you to know. They used you for their own purposes, manipulated you . . . lied to you."

"No," he shouted, though he knew it was true.

"You are young, well-intentioned, a bit naive. They counted on that, exploited it." He paused to let the impact of his words penetrate. "And now they've abandoned you. There's no one to help you, Steve, no possibility of rescue from the outside. You're quite alone."

Steve thought about the supposed plan to get him out, if

arrested. Mike had never explained it. He crossed his legs, holding his thighs tight together. Pressure had built in his bladder; he was afraid he'd lose control of it. "I want to speak to the American ambassador."

"He can't help you!" the interrogator said angrily. "No one can help you. You're to be put on trial, sentenced, and sent to prison." Prestin leaned forward on the table. "Unless you cooperate. If you cooperate I may be able to help you. What happened to Susan?"

"Nothing. I don't know. When I got back to the hotel she was gone. She probably went for a walk."

Prestin came closer, lowering his face into Barth's. Steve could taste his breath, the foul odor. "The State Prosecutor is upstairs readying your case for trial. I have the authority to stop him. But I'll do nothing unless I have the information I want. Susan Stern . . . where did she go when she left the hotel?"

"I don't know. We made love. She fell asleep and I went for a walk. When I returned she was gone."

"Come on, Steve. You're going to have to do better than that. We know she told you where she was going."

"She didn't. I swear. You have to believe me. She didn't say anything. She was asleep when I left the Metropole." He tugged at the soaked handkerchief.

"You want me to believe that you two traveled to Russia together on a mission for the Zionists and that on your first afternoon in Moscow you just left her in the hotel sleeping?"

"Yes," he said, half hysterical.

"Please, Steve, I'm not that naive. Don't lie to me. Where did Susan go?"

"I don't know. I *don't* know . . . that's the truth. You have to believe me. I knew nothing about all this. They used me, you said so yourself. They didn't tell me anything. Susan didn't tell me anything. She was asleep, then she was gone. Please, I'm telling you what I know."

The interrogator circled the table and sat down across from Barth. The boy looked exhausted; the fear in his eyes stark naked, real. Yet he was sticking to his story. Suddenly Nikolai Petrovich Prestin wondered if he was being duped, if the boy was a practiced professional like the girl, feigning innocence to fool him.

"Barth," he shouted. "Who killed Susan Stern?"

"What!" His lips whitened, his mouth quivered. He stared blankly at the Russian. What had he said? Someone had killed Susan? She was dead? He could hear his own voice in the distance, asking the questions.

"Who killed her, Barth?"

"Killed her . . ." He laughed hysterically. "You've been keeping me here, asking me questions about Susan . . . and the whole time, she was dead and you said nothing." Moisture rose in his eyes but the tears wouldn't fall. He looked away. How much time had passed? A few hours. They had been together, talking about their past, inside each other. She had touched him, clawed through the barrier that protected him from pain yet at the same time invited it. And now she was . . . He screamed.

Colonel Grigorenko rose and left the room. The news of the girl's death had been too much for the boy. He was near collapse. The interrogation would have to be halted—temporarily.

Slowly Grigorenko made his way through the light green corridors of the eight-story structure built by the Rossiya Insurance Company in 1897 and appropriated by the architects of the Revolution two decades later. Reaching the First Directorate's wing, he brushed past Yuri Pirozhkov and entered Zavorin's office without knocking. It was late at night and he wasn't in the mood for protocol. As he stepped from the brown parquet wood onto the blue and gold patterned Oriental rug resentment born of jealousy scraped his nerves. He wanted this office and he wanted Zavorin pushed into his.

"Well, Petr Dmitrivich," the Major General said, leaning forward on his elbows as Grigorenko lowered himself into the seat opposite the desk. "What did he tell you?"

"Nothing. The boy is either very stubborn or very innocent."

Zavorin rose and paced to the window and back. "What in the hell have you imbeciles done? Who killed the girl? Somebody in your department? The GRU? Kuznetsov and the Second Chief Directorate? I want to know . . . and I want to know now!"

"I've checked every possibility, Comrade General, and drawn a blank."

"Then check again, you fool. Somebody in this city killed her and I want to know who. If a member of the KGB is attempting a power play to thwart this operation and embarrass me I want him crushed. Is that clear?" Zavorin dropped into his seat. "Where was the body found?"

"The black Zaporozhets was parked on the bank of the Moskva River not far from the Khoroshovo-Mnevniki housing compound. Susan was in the back seat. There's positive evidence of an artificially set explosion. She was immolated."

"You're certain it was the same car that picked her up in Hermitage Park?" Zavorin asked.

"Yes. The license numbers match. The doctors examined the remains and verified they belonged to a female in her early twenties. Moreover, the identification necklace she wore was only partially melted. The name Susan was still legible."

"I assume the Zaporozhets was stolen."

Grigorenko nodded. "I ordered a security report on the owner anyway."

"Good." Zavorin's face lost some of its anger. "I don't understand what happened, Petr Dmitrivich. Who could have done it?"

Grigorenko shrugged. "Maybe the Americans . . ."

"I don't think so. Why would the CIA kill one of its own? For what purpose?"

"MI-5?"

"The same problem. Both services are capable of eliminating their own operatives—for a reason. But we have no reason. What would the British possibly gain by killing the girl?"

"Revenge against the Americans for some double-cross." Grigorenko lit a French Gauloise. "Maybe they killed the girl here to remove suspicion from themselves and implicate us."

"It's a possibility, but the British rarely operate that way. It lacks a certain style they demand."

Grigorenko sat back in the soft chair. "It seems, then, that we are at an impasse. The boy certainly didn't do it."

Zavorin rose and began to pace again. "No, the microdots we recovered from the books they brought Zaretsky state clearly that the girl was a CIA agent and the boy a pawn picked up in Jerusalem. He couldn't have anything to do with the killing. Besides, I think he was falling for her."

"I agree," Grigorenko said, anxious to terminate the conversation and return home. The back of his neck ached and he wanted some milk to quiet his ulcer.

Zavorin stopped and stared at his subordinate, his face hard.

"Colonel, I want you to drop everything else. Find out exactly what happened to the girl—who killed her, how, and why. And I don't want the information next week. Do you understand?"

"Yes."

"Start with the boy. Use every means available. *Every.* He must know something."

Grigorenko rose to leave. "You'll have his full statement tomorrow."

"Good."

Grigorenko pulled the door open, then stopped and turned. "General, why don't we just crush the Jewish dissidents? We have the men and the means to do it."

Zavorin looked up impatiently. "They serve a purpose, Petr Dmitrivich. The Jewish movement in Russia is what the Communist Party in the United States was to the FBI in the fifties—an organization to be sustained in order to infiltrate."

Grigorenko nodded and moved out the door. In Zavorin's outer office he picked up the phone and dialed a seldom-used number. The Major General had said every means available. After a brief conversation, he proceeded down the deserted and dimly lit corridor toward the interrogation chambers.

Nikolai Petrovich Prestin was leaning against the green wall outside the room, smoking.

Grigorenko's facial expression told him that the Fifth Directorate Colonel had been verbally assaulted. Earlier, he, too, had been called into Zavorin's office and yelled at for a full half hour. It seemed to Prestin that Zavorin was responding excessively to the incident. An American agent had been killed, not one of theirs. It was almost as if the Major General was attempting to hide something by overreacting. He should be pleased the girl was dead.

With any luck her murder would help freeze the thaw in the Cold War he was known to oppose so strongly. Suddenly something clicked in Prestin's head. It was just possible that Zavorin had ordered the girl murdered himself.

Soon Grigorenko and he were joined by a third man, who followed them into the interrogation chamber.

Steve lay slumped on the table, head folded in his arms. At the sound of the door opening he looked up. He saw the same two men as before and somebody else—a tall, dark-haired man with a large nose and blotched skin. He glared at Steve and shouted something in Russian.

"Get up!" Prestin translated.

Steve jumped to his feet.

"Turn around! Stop! State your name."

"Steven Barth."

"Sit down," the man barked. "You will answer my questions."

Steve nodded, trembling, as the translation reached him.

"Were you told to disguise yourself in any way?"

"No," he said, shaking his head. "Look at me—blond hair, red beard, and Western clothing. I don't look Russian."

"Were you told to watch for anyone following you?"

"What for? Why would anybody want to follow me?"

"Do you know Hebrew?" he asked, seemingly ignoring the boy's answers.

"No," Steve said quickly, drawing on some source of strength he didn't know existed—a final, thin barrier stretched across the truth. "You see, when a Jewish boy is thirteen he has a ceremony called a Bar Mitzvah. I went to Sunday school for a year to learn to read from the Torah, that's the first part of the Bible, but I really didn't . . ."

Abruptly moving close, the tall man struck Barth across the face with the back of his palm. "Shut up!" he shouted. The blood flowed into Steve's cheek, bringing sharp pain.

Behind them, out of Barth's view, Nikolai Prestin raised his hand requesting that his colleague, who had been masquerading as a prosecutor, leave the room. Then he spoke softly, his voice sounding sympathetic and understanding to the terrified boy slumped in the chair three feet from him.

"Steve, I know you never intended to get involved in this business. I understand what has happened to you. There's nothing I want more than to send you home. If you tell us everything I promise I will do what I can to persuade the Prosecutor not to bring you to trial. But I must warn you. According to Article 182 of the Soviet Criminal Code, evading or incompletely answering a question is punishable by imprisonment. If you continue to refuse to cooperate . . ." He let the sentence hang. "I'm the only one who can help you. The Israelis and the Americans don't care. They'll claim they never heard of you, say you came to Russia on your own. You'll rot in a dark cell, forgotten, while they recruit another innocent victim to take your place."

Steve squeezed his eyes. He felt each pulsation of his blood singly, at regular intervals. Reality and the world of lies melded. They had used him in England and Israel, told him nothing, introduced Susan as *his* companion. But they wouldn't abandon him, let him go to trial, watch him sentenced to prison, and do nothing.

Or would they? Sweat broke out on his forehead and back and suddenly he felt cold.

"Tell me, when did you first meet Susan?" the interrogator pressed.

"I can't. I'm tired. Let me go back to the hotel. I can't think now."

"Just tell me about Susan. Then you'll have a bed and something hot to eat. You met her in London, right?"

"Yes."

"You two became lovers?"

"No. Nothing happened in England. Nothing. Not until last . . . this afternoon."

"You cared about her and she about you. We know that."

He nodded, convincing himself the wish was the reality. Sleeping with him couldn't have been an assignment. She wasn't using him.

"You two were close. Strangers thrown together in a foreign country, you talked a lot, shared intimacies. Maybe about past relationships." Prestin was drawing on the text transcribed from the listening devices in their hotel room.

"Yes," he said.

"You spent a lot of time walking around Moscow, seeing the sights, talking. You were together for twenty-four hours, never apart. Think back. She must have said or done something that hinted at where she was going when she left the hotel. We want her murderer, Steve. We want to punish him for what he did to Susan. He does not deserve to remain free. He raped her, mutilated the body, and dumped it in the mud at the edge of the Moskva River," Prestin lied.

"No." An image of Susan, disfigured, rose in his mind. He buried his head in his hands, pushed the image away, trying to focus on the blackness, but she reappeared instantly.

"Help us, Steve. Help us find her murderer. Where did she go when she left the hotel?"

"I don't know."

"Who did she go to meet?"

"I've already told you. I don't know. I'm exhausted. Why won't you believe me?"

"What did she say before she left the hotel? What excuse did she give you?"

"None." His breathing was labored. The air he drew into his lungs seemed thick and heavy. He looked at the face of his interrogator, blurred in the bright light. "Susan fell asleep so I went out for a walk." It was difficult to talk; he had to force the words out. "When I got back to the hotel she was gone. She didn't leave a note. She couldn't tell me anything because I wasn't there!"

"I'm afraid if you continue like this I won't be able to have any influence on the Prosecutor." Prestin stepped back out of the light, softening his voice. "You're so young. I don't want you to spend the next fifteen years in a prison cell. I prefer to help you. Let me. Who were you told to contact if you got in trouble? Who did Susan go to see?"

"I don't know anything! I don't. I don't."

"Empty your pockets," the interrogator said suddenly.

Steve froze, then panic tore through him. Zev's letter! He could feel it outlined against his pants. He couldn't place it in the hands of the KGB.

"Your pockets, empty them. Now," came the harsh commands.

Shaking, Steve put his wallet, comb, pen, and a few coins on the table. Maybe they wouldn't search him, wouldn't make him turn over the letter.

Prestin took the wallet, thumbed through the contents, then

placed it back on the table. Circling closer to Steve, he examined the boy's clothing, saw the slight bulge in his pants. "There's something in your left rear pocket. Remove what's there."

"No," Steve said, fear glassy in his eyes.

"Let me have it!" Prestin shouted.

Silent, Steve huddled against himself—his head pounding, his mouth dry.

"Empty that pocket or I'll have the pants ripped off you!"

He had to give it to them. He had no choice. They'd take it anyway. The despair of total defeat kicked him in the face. He thrust his hand in his pocket and threw the envelope on the table. Prestin withdrew the sheet of paper it contained and read quietly.

"Suppose we say you gave this to me voluntarily," he said.

Steve shook his head weakly. "No." It took all his strength to manage the word.

Prestin smiled and handed the letter to Grigorenko, who, sitting silently through the questioning, gave no indication that he understood English. As he read the page the interrogator pushed Steve's wallet toward him. Steve replaced it mechanically. His motor movements seemed disconnected from his brain; his mind kept repeating that he'd betrayed Zev. He should have found a safe place to hide the envelope.

"Take him away," Grigorenko said in Russian after finishing the letter. "We can continue this in the morning." Tired, he wanted to return home for the milk his stomach required. They'd been at it for hours; it was late, and it didn't appear Barth was going to tell them anything. He would let the boy alone for a while, allowing his thoughts, the fear of isolation, and the night to do the interrogator's work for him. Besides, continuing was pointless; he knew Barth was telling the truth.

As the boy was led from the room Grigorenko lit a Gauloise. After a few quick puffs he threw the cigarette on the floor without bothering to extinguish it. The hours spent in questioning the boy had brought him no closer to the girl's murderer, while Zavorin's implied threat hung over his head like the blade of a guillotine.

A plainclothes officer led Steve through the series of doors and corridors and out into the cold night. An unmarked Volga was idling against the curb, white exhaust rising from the tailpipe. It was the only sound, anywhere. Steve settled into the back of the car with a new escort and leaned on the far door.

The driver pulled into the empty street and they proceeded out of Dzerzhinsky Square. Steve was too exhausted to care where they were going.

After a short ride that seemed interminable the driver deposited his passengers in front of the Metropole Hotel. The plainclothesman led Steve through the lobby and into the elevator, whose silent operator carried them up to the fifth floor. At the end of the corridor the officer inserted a key in the lock and pushed the heavy door open with his foot. The room was windowless and small, with a narrow bed, wood floor, sink, and chest of drawers. Steve's belongings were stacked neatly in one corner against the wall. There was no sign of Susan's clothes.

"The bathroom is directly across the hall," the policeman said, in heavily accented English. Turning, he headed for the door. "Someone will come for you in the morning." And he was gone.

Steve watched the door close behind him, staring at it for a long time. Then he sank down on the edge of the bed. It was hard. He sat there, rigid. The silence in the room filled his ears. It pressed in from the walls, growing louder and louder.

"Susan." He called out her name, shattering the soundless whirl around him. "How can you be dead? How in the hell can you really be dead?" He fell on his side and slammed his fist into the mattress. He cared, had begun to fall in love with her. Why could he admit it to himself now, when it was too late? He crushed the pillow in his arms, pretending it was her.

The minutes clung to each other, one only reluctantly giving way to the next. Steve shut his eyes, wanting very much to cry but unable to. Then, slowly, an idea forced its way into his mind. As it cleared consciousness he held onto it, refusing to let go. There was a possibility, however slight, that Susan wasn't dead. The KGB might be manipulating him for some reason, making it look like she was dead in order to break him. He sat up excitedly. That was it. Susan was being held at another location. They were chipping at his resistance, insuring that he felt terrified, alone. They wanted something. When he was sufficiently weakened the interrogator would pounce, turning away from Susan to the real reason they had arrested him. It would come at an unexpected moment. He got up and paced nervously toward the door and back. He would have to prepare himself. When the shift in the interrogation came he'd be ready to parry it. They would get nothing out of him. Eventually they'd see that and let him go. Then he'd take Susan and . . .

He stopped midway between bed and wall, and bit his lower lip. Who was he kidding? He knew nothing. The Soviets couldn't be setting him up. Susan was a CIA agent, killed for some unknown reason. He was the last link to her. All they wanted to know was who killed her and why.

"They've got to be reasonable," Steve said out loud, vaguely aware that he was talking to a listening device. "It's so clear, they've got to understand. I didn't know. I can't tell them any-thing. Once they see that they'll let me go. I'm certain they will. They believe me." His eyes searched for a microphone. "I know they do."

Silence.

Kicking off his shoes, he dropped onto the bed. The tiredness invaded every muscle of his body. His eyelids closed. He hung suspended between thoughts and dreams—then lost conscious-ness.

The hours wore away. Scenes played in his mind, bizarre disconnected vignettes: his parents being beaten and tortured by the CIA because of his arrest; Dahlia, his old Israeli girlfriend, in a KGB uniform grilling him about his indifference; David, Michael, and Wulf in London drinking a toast to his captivity. Then he was in a dark basement, moving against the wall, unseen. In the center of the room was a gurney, a sheet draped over its sides. He listened, heard nothing, and inched away from the wall. Taking a corner of the sheet in one hand, he slowly pulled it to the floor, revealing Susan's naked body. He undressed and climbed over her.

Steve strained to wake up. He was practiced in tearing him-self out of nightmares; they had plagued him regularly, since Johnny Robinson's death. Sometimes by a strong act of will he managed to escape, to pull himself out of the dream by his own efforts. But this time he did not succeed. The interrogation had exhausted him. He sweated and panted in his sleep. The dream went on.

Reaching down, he moved one leg to the side. Her flesh felt cold, her limb rigid. It resisted movement. He closed his eyes and pushed the other leg to the side, wanting to stop but unable to, the same way he had been unable to cry. He looked at her face. Her skin was pale and chalky. No breath passed her lips.

Steve struggled to wake up.

He lowered himself slowly, cautiously, onto the inert body. The tip of his flesh touched her . . .

He screamed, bolting up, awake. For a moment he didn't remember where he was. Then everything came back to him. Drying his forehead and the back of his neck with the pillowcase, he realized, to his dismay, that he was fully clothed. He stood up and headed toward the door, vaguely aware that he'd escaped a nightmare. The details of the dream were gone—what remained was the fear. Though he did know he'd screamed, he didn't remember why.

Morning light falling through the bathroom window glinted off the white walls, hurting Steve's eyes. There were two stalls to the right, rectangular with wooden partitions. Steve pushed the door on the first one. Hinges squeaking, it opened. He lowered himself onto the cold seat and shivered. If he ever got out of there— He felt himself sweat. He wiped his forehead with a sheet of toilet paper. Taking a breath, he placed both hands on the sides of the stall. There was a pain in his stomach. He leaned against the partition, his eyes following a crack in the wall. It looked like a face, like . . .

"Steve," a voice spoke softly in Hebrew from the next stall, "are you all right?"

"What?" he said, staring at the wood partition.

"It's Andrei. I've been waiting for you. Are you okay?"

"Andrei," Steve said, ripping at the toilet paper. "Yes, yes, I'm fine." He struggled to pull his pants up. "How did you know I was here?"

"The elevator operator is Jewish. He told us you were arrested and brought back to the hotel. Zev sent me to find out what happened."

"I don't know what happened," Steve said, his voice constricted. "I was in the room waiting for Susan and the next thing I knew there was a knock on the door, three men entered, and took me to KGB headquarters. They said I was under arrest."

"There are a lot of people very grateful for those Hebrew books." Andrei's tone was comforting. "They'll do anything. How can we help?"

"Telephone the American ambassador and tell him I'm being held. They won't let me contact him."

"Done. What else?"

"I don't know. They questioned me until late last night and the interrogator said he would continue this morning. They threatened to put me on trial."

"Try not to worry," Andrei said gently. "They just want to scare you into talking. In this era of detente the Soviets are very concerned about their relationship with the United States. They won't do anything to jeopardize their chances to receive trade credits. They'll probably question you for a few hours, then put you on a plane to London. Concentrate on that and try to relax as much as possible."

"I'll try."

"Good." Andrei paused for a moment. "Steve, what about the things we gave you in the apartment? Do you still have them?"

"No." Steve's tone was anxious. "I'm sorry. Zev's letter was in my pocket. The interrogator tried to make me give it to him voluntarily. I refused, but he took it from me anyway. I couldn't help it. I had no choice."

"I see . . . and the book?"

"The book. I don't know. I hid it in my hotel room under my clothes. Nobody's mentioned it. Maybe they didn't find it."

"Possible, but unlikely. A thorough search of your room would be mandatory under the circumstances. The KGB would not miss a large object hidden in such an obvious place."

"You're right," Steve said, feeling foolish for having put the Bible where he did. "Then why didn't they say anything about it?"

"Patience, my friend. The secret police are very thorough. They will confront you with the book when they are ready."

Steve put his hand on the wood partition, wanting very much to reach through the wall and touch his friend—the only thing he wanted more was to salvage some small part of the mission. "Maybe I'll be able to convince them that the book is mine. There's no evidence to show that it was printed in Russia. If I demand that they let me keep it, threaten to go to the Western press with a story about how the Soviets confiscate Bibles from tourists, maybe they won't take it from me. Then you could meet me in Jerusalem and I could give it to you as planned."

"You can try," Andrei said, with little hope in his voice. "Who knows, you might even succeed."

"I will." Steve stiffened with determination. He now had a goal, a psychological rope to hold on to during the interrogation. He would not let go of it—no matter what they did to him.

Andrei shifted position in the small space. "I can't stay much longer. It's dangerous for me to be here."

"Wait," Steve said, desperate, not wanting him to leave. The prospect of returning alone to his room was terrifying. "Andrei, they told me Susan's been killed."

He heard the sound of a fist striking the wall. "Oh, no. How?"

"I don't know. The interrogator told me her body was dumped in the Moskva River."

"Those bastards." Anger etched his words. "Who did it?"

"Nobody seems to know. My interrogator keeps claiming that Susan told me where she was going before she left the hotel, but she didn't."

"I see."

"She fell asleep so I went for a walk. When I got back to the room she was gone."

"She said nothing about who she was going to meet?"

"Nothing. I expected her to be in the room when I returned."

"Did she give you any hint that she was going out?"

"None. She was sound asleep when I left the hotel." Or was she? Steve wondered suddenly. Susan had initiated their lovemaking. Maybe it had all been an act, a cover to screen other motives. If she had plans to meet someone she could have set up the entire afternoon, feigned sleep to get him out of the room, allowing her to proceed alone to a rendezvous point. No, it couldn't have been like that, he told himself, fighting the nagging feeling that it was.

"The KGB must have killed her," Andrei said, after a moment. "They'll probably try to cover themselves by implicating you. They're fully capable of planting enough evidence to make it appear you murdered her."

"But nobody will believe that. We were lovers. I had no motive." The words raced out of his mouth.

"Nobody has to believe it. All the Soviets need do is surround your actions with enough doubt to create the possibility that in the heat of a lover's quarrel you killed her. Casting suspicion on you should be enough to take the edge off American outrage."

"What will happen to me?"

"Probably nothing. I suspect they'll keep the interrogation going for a while, then expel you from the country."

Steve gulped for air.

"Now, you'd better go back across the hall," Andrei said. "Your captors will become suspicious if you remain here too long. I wouldn't like them to come looking for you and find me."

Steve buckled his pants and took a last look at the crack in the ceiling. "I understand." He put one hand on the door and stopped. "Andrei, thanks for coming." His voice was weak. "You have no idea how much it helped . . . to speak to someone."

"Hurry now," Andrei said. "I'll call the American Embassy as soon as I leave the hotel."

Steve pressed his hand on the wall between them. "Goodbye," he said. After hesitating a final moment he headed for his room.

As Steve stepped into the hallway, a door at the end of the corridor opened just enough so that the man standing behind it could watch the movement before him. He had been standing there for some time, waiting for the boy to leave the bathroom. His legs were tired and his back ached from the position he'd assumed leaning against the door, listening. But Dmitri Karpov was a patient man. Years as a field agent had taught him the art of waiting. He lived in his mind, not his body. There he viewed a constant series of options and alternatives, testing plans and weighing proposals. He maneuvered agents and innocents as he would actors on a stage. As Steve returned to his room Karpov massaged the back of his neck with one hand. He found physical discomfort a minor inconvenience. He was never bored.

Soon another man stepped into the hallway and as he moved

toward the elevator Karpov edged his door shut, lest he be observed. He recognized the man's face. It belonged to Andrei Bukharov, one of the Hebrew teachers.

Andrei entered the eastern edge of Sverdlov Square, proceeding past the long and sober facade of the Maly Theater, past the stone statue of Ostrovsky, the author of *The Storm*, which was first performed at the Maly. Though Andrei wanted to make a phone call immediately, he hurried by the phone booth at the corner of Ulitza Petrovka. He was still too close to the Metropole. The KGB, knowing that trained amateurs sent to contact dissident intellectuals like Sakharov, Amalrik, and Orlov were told not to use their hotel room phones, monitored the pay telephones within a five-block radius of all Intourist hotels. The information they reaped from this ploy was most helpful.

Andrei skirted a long line of people waiting to buy the morning *Pravda*, and headed toward the phone box in Trubnaya Square. He did not notice the man following him.

Steve walked across the hall, closed the door behind him, and leaned back against the hard wood, listening to the sound of his own breathing. Everything would be all right now. Andrei would contact the American ambassador and a representative from the embassy would demand to see him. The Soviets would be forced to comply. Then they would have to let him go.

His eyes moved around the room. He'd have to find something to do until then, something to keep his mind away from his thoughts. He followed the cracks in the ceiling, imagining they were rivers flowing through the Midwest. The largest one was the Mississippi. He was in a canoe dodging the rapids. The water was rushing around him. The air was cold. He looked into the stream.

Water churned in foamy whirlpools. In the nearest one a face appeared, blurred, then sharpened. It was a girl. Susan. He shut his eyes. The river disappeared.

The phone rang, the strident sound shaking him. He ran toward the end table and lifted the receiver, leaving a sweaty imprint on the plastic. Unable to say hello, he listened.

"Mr. Barth."

"Yes."

"This is Nikolai Petrovich Prestin. May I visit you?"

Steve hesitated. "Yes," he said finally.

Steve lowered the phone. He wondered why his interrogator had requested permission to see him.

Momentarily there was a knock on the door. Steve stood and waited for the man to enter. He didn't. Instead a voice spoke from the hallway.

"May I come in?"

"Of course." Steve crossed the room, pulled the door open, and faced the heavy-chested, pale Russian. Prestin wore the same masked smile Steve had seen when he was first ushered into his presence at KGB headquarters.

"The Prosecutor has reviewed the statement you gave last night and has prepared some further questions which we request you answer now. Is that satisfactory?"

Steve nodded wearily.

"Can I call the American Embassy first?"

"They can do nothing to help you, Steve. You have broken Soviet law. If I was traveling in the United States and I violated your laws the Russian Embassy would be powerless. Ignorance of a law is no excuse. It is your responsibility to abide by the statutes of the country you are visiting."

Steve sat on the edge of the bed, all hope resting with Andrei. He said nothing.

Prestin pulled a chair away from the wall and made himself comfortable. "How much were you paid to come to Russia?" he asked, lighting a dark Cuban cigar.

"Paid?" Steve said. "For coming here? Why would anyone give me money to have a few conversations with some Russian Jews?"

"Then you were doing it for idealism."

Steve lacked the strength to argue. "Yes."

"What instructions were you given about talking inside your hotel room?" Prestin asked.

"None," Steve lied. Cigar smoke filled the uncirculated air giving Steve a headache that pressed in from the corners of his temples. "Why would Susan and I not want to talk in our room?"

"Were you told to watch for people following you in the street?"

"No. I don't understand. What are you getting at?" He couldn't concentrate, his temples pulsed.

Prestin let out a sigh. "You know, after such nice summer days, the cold we had last night hit me like a *zets in the kishkeys*."

"What did you say?" Steve stalled, then managed to collect his thoughts. "I don't understand Russian."

"That's Yiddish, not Russian," he laughed. "It means like . . . like . . ." He fumbled for words. "Like a kick in the balls." He laughed louder. "Your parents don't speak Yiddish?"

"No, they were born in America."

"Yiddish is a wonderful language, but like any language, slang is most important to learn, *na'chon*?"

"Could you repeat that?" Steve asked nervously. "I didn't

understand the last word." Jumping immediately from Yiddish to the Hebrew equivalent for "right," Prestin had caught him off guard. He had almost responded.

"You don't speak Hebrew?" Prestin said, smiling superciliously. He lifted his hand and snapped his fingers. "I speak it fluently. *A'nee korai tanach*." He pointed proudly to his chest. "Do you know what that means?"

"*A'nee* is I, *korai* is read," Steve answered slowly, attempting to calm himself. "But what is *ta-ta-nick*?"

"*Tanach*," he corrected. "*Tanach* is the Bible. You don't know that?"

"No," Steve said.

The phone rang. Prestin answered it and listened for a long time without speaking, which gave Steve the impression that their conversation was being monitored and that his interrogator was being given further instructions. After a short "*Da*," Prestin cradled the receiver and returned to his chair.

"You have committed a serious crime against the Soviet people," the Russian said in an admonishing tone. "You have entered the Soviet Union as a guest and meddled in her internal affairs, and you have been consorting with known hooligans." He ground his cigar against the arm of the chair burning a ring in the wood. Then he swept the ashes and cinder to the floor. "But because you are young, inexperienced, and obviously unaware of the seriousness of what you were doing, the Prosecutor has decided to be merciful."

"Thank you," Steve said.

He smiled. "There is one thing, though, that we should discuss. You are not planning to go to the FBI and tell them what happened to you here, are you?" He grimaced as if he had eaten a

116

bitter piece of fruit. "They will cause you much trouble, run you around from office to office, make you sign statements and give endless hours of testimony."

"I just want you to let me go," Steve said, his voice weak. "I never want to think about Russia again."

"Everybody's been very polite to you here, haven't they? Nobody has harmed or struck you?"

Steve remembered the blow the Prosecutor gave him. "No. Everybody's been quite nice. Thank you very much."

"Good," Prestin said, abruptly stern. "Then I will not expect any newspaper articles or stories to be written about you, about how you were tortured in the Soviet Union. Because if I do see such a story or anything written in which your name appears, you should know that the KGB can find you anywhere in the world, and the next time we meet we will not be so humanistic. Do you understand?"

Steve nodded, terrified.

"Pile your belongings on the bed."

Steve hurried to where his clothes had been stacked next to his empty suitcase. Lifting several pairs of shirts and pants in both hands, he stopped, rigid. On the floor, on top of the rest of his clothes, was Andrei's Bible! For a painful instant he considered trying to hide it; but he couldn't, the interrogator was watching every move he made. His hands began to shake—he gripped the shirts tighter. But there was nothing he could do. On his next trip he laid the Bible along with *The Hobbit* and his *Star Trek* scripts beside the clothes. A few minutes later everything had been transferred to the bed.

Nikolai Petrovich Prestin rose slowly and began rummaging through Steve's belongings. He picked up the English books and searched the pages, holding each in turn to the bare bulb hanging from a cord in the center of the ceiling. It had been an old trick of Lenin's, still practiced in the covert world of spies, to write sensitive information across the pages of a book with milk. The liquid dries invisible to all but the trained eye and remains so until placed in contact with a hot iron. The scorched milk turns brown and is easily read. Satisfied, Prestin tossed the paperbacks back on the bed and turned to the worn Hebrew text.

"What do we have here?" he asked mockingly.

"A Bible."

Prestin held the front cover and shook the book, tearing the binding. Nothing fell out. He thumbed the pages, laughing. "Are you sure there aren't secret messages hidden in here?"

Steve remained silent.

"Give me your tickets and passport," Prestin said, closing the book.

Steve took the documents from a corner of the bed and thrust them into his palm.

Prestin showed a slight smile. "Funny, you claim you don't know Hebrew, yet you're carrying a Hebrew Bible."

Steve panicked. The Russian didn't believe the book was his. He had to convince him, for Andrei. "I lied about the Hebrew," he blurted out. "Please, I wasn't trying to trick you. I got scared and I thought . . ."

"What else did you lie about?" Prestin asked fiercely.

"Nothing." Steve's voice shook. "Nothing, I swear."

"We will see." Prestin threw the book on the floor. "Now, please pack your bags and wait. You are being transferred." The Russian turned on his heels and left the room.

Steve stood there, the luxury of hope ripped from him. He

thought Prestin wanted his tickets in order to arrange a flight to the West. Picking up the Bible, he dropped into the chair. His mind turned to Susan.

An hour and a half later there was an incisive knock on the door. Steve got up from the bed and noticed that his suitcase, though he didn't remember packing, was closed and on the floor. Before he could open the door Prestin and the Prosecutor entered.

"Stand at attention!" Prestin shouted.

The Prosecutor extracted a piece of paper from his inside coat pocket and drilled a glare at the boy's frightened eyes.

"The Prosecutor will read a statement and I will translate," Prestin said loudly.

Steve nodded. The Prosecutor began to mumble in Russian.

"The Central Committee of the Communist Party of Moscow decrees that due to the mercy and compassion of the Soviet State, it has been decided not to bring the accused, Steven Barth, to trial for crimes wantonly committed against the Soviet peoples. . . ." The Prosecutor was reading faster than Prestin could translate, causing the interrogator to stumble. Finally, frustrated by his inability to express the required technical terms in English and the lack of time, Prestin broke off and said, "You're kicked out of the country."

Steve stared at him, disbelieving.

The Prosecutor disappeared out the door while Prestin handed his prisoner his passport and tickets. "Take your things and let's go," he ordered.

Outside it had been raining. They entered a waiting Volga sedan and sped out Ulitza Petrovka toward the green-ring boulevards. Clouds moved across the gray sky. A few drops fell on the windshield. But the rain, exhausted after a violent downpour, had ceased.

In the front seat Prestin withdrew a small piece of paper from his wallet and handed it to Steve. "This is for you."

"What is it?" The form was printed and filled out in Russian.

"Your hotel bill, eleven rubles for last night. You can pay it when you exchange your currency at the airport."

Steve dropped deeper into the seat. "But our room was prepaid," he said helplessly.

"This one wasn't. If you prefer staying in Moscow, refuse to pay it."

Steve folded the note, repeatedly creasing the edges with his fingernails. He rarely vented his anger, choosing instead to hold back, telling himself when on the verge of an outburst that each individual affront was not that important—which really meant, he felt he wasn't that important.

On Leningradskoye Highway the Volga picked up speed. Towering pines rose on each side of the road, their needles and cones covering the black earth. Steve rolled down the window. The rain had washed the air; the breeze carried the damp aroma of mint.

At Sheremetyevo Airport Steve's companion bypassed the waiting lines and moved immediately to the clerks deciding their countrymen's fates at passport control, currency control, and customs—mini-dictators who inflict inconvenience and hardship, apparently as a way of retaliating for the misery and frustration they suffer.

At the boarding gate Prestin stopped and pointed down the walkway leading toward an Aeroflot TU-114 passenger plane. "I hope you enjoyed your stay in the Soviet Union," he said. "Have a safe journey. The other passengers have already boarded." He left without waiting for a response.

Steve walked to the end of the passageway, pushed the glass door open, and stepped outside. Eyes on the tarmac, he moved toward the boarding ramp. A soldier in his green uniform and high boots, armed with a hip pistol and a Kalashnikov AK-47, stood beneath the tail of the jet and another, similarly armed, waited by the ramp. They were watching not for terrorists but for stowaways to the West.

Steve climbed the stairs slowly. Inside the plane he was guided to one of the many empty seats and instructed by the Aeroflot stewardess to fasten his safety belt. Moments later the engines revved into a high-pitched whine and the plane began to taxi toward the runway. As the heavy jet lifted into the air Steve stared straight ahead.

From the seat across the aisle Dmitri Karpov looked out the window and smiled.

Nine-Jerusalem

The number eighteen bus slammed to a halt across from Yafo Gate, pitching the passengers forward. The Colonel rose and slowly made his way down the back stairs.

Across the wide plaza stood the Old City, its secluded quarters and hidden passageways girdled by a high belt of stone. As the Colonel moved toward the open gate he glimpsed the Tower of David and the domes of Old Jerusalem's churches and synagogues—all protected by the walls of Suleiman the Magnificent. Sennacherib and Nebuchadnezzar, Ptolemy and Herod, Titus and the Crusaders of Godfrey de Bouillon, Tamerlane and the Saracens of Saladin, all had fought, burned, and killed here, committing crimes in the name of religion.

The Colonel entered the Street of David. The narrow vaulted alleyway was blocked by long dresses hanging in the air and cluttered on the ground with copper trays, sheshbesh boards, handcarved tables, and colorful Arab rugs. Displayed behind glass windows were cheap olivewood camels, mother-of-pearl boxes, and turquoise jewelry, arranged around a seemingly infinite variety of crosses and Stars of David. Old men, their black and white checkered keffiyehs flowing from their shoulders, sat on stone steps drawing smoke from the tubes of waterpipes while their sons and grandsons enticed passers-by into the shops with the offer of free coffee and the promise of "No charge for looking." It saddened the Colonel to see the once proud Jerusalem Arabs exchanging their dignity for the tourist dollar; then again, he reminded himself, they were only imitating the Israeli shopkeepers in the New City.

As the alley narrowed and sloped down, becoming the Street of the Chain, the stench of spoiled food, trapped by the roof overhead, soured the air. From niches on both sides of the passageway merchants beckoned shoppers to pick from the mounds of eggplant, olives, sticky raisins, cabbage, and cucumbers piled on the wood stalls before them. Rotting tomatoes and avocados, tossed on the floor, attracted buzzing flies. Farther down, just before the street turned and opened into the spacious square below the Western Wall and the Mosque of Omar, sides of raw meat hung in the open air across from racks of sheepskin coats. At the end of the passageway two Israeli soldiers armed with short-muzzled Uzi submachine guns searched all bags and packages for bombs before they allowed access to the sacred sites.

At the top of the Street of the Chain the Colonel turned left into the dark Suq el Khawajat, leading toward the Church of the Holy Sepulchre. He passed short-sleeved Israelis, a mix of modern and traditionally attired Arab men, and Arab women all wearing the same, long, covering dresses. At the end of the market next to a shoe store redolent with the odor of raw leather was a small glass-fronted café. The Colonel ducked inside, moved to a table in the center of the near-empty room, and sat next to the man waiting there for him.

"How was your flight, Joseph?" the head of Israeli Intelligence asked.

"On time."

The Colonel nodded, motioned to the waiter, and ordered Turkish coffee. "You saw Michael Marks in London?"

"Briefly."

"Did he send a message for me?"

"No."

The Colonel's coffee arrived and he sprinkled two spoonfuls of large granulated sugar into the handleless cup without mixing it. He didn't want the sediment at the bottom to rise.

Joseph Eliav was the Colonel's top European field agent. A man of fifty-five, the head of a large London-based travel firm, he had been recruited by the Colonel late in life, at the age of forty-eight. In the days of the British mandate he had been a Haganah officer and he was still disciplined and deceptive. Unlike many of the Colonel's operatives, he showed no signs of the stress that seemed to cripple most career agents as they looked back on their fiftieth birthdays. He had spent twenty rich years in the fields of Kibbutz Regavim, near Caesarea, the ancient capital of the Romans in Palestine. The last quarter of that period was passed pleasantly in the kibbutz greenhouse, cultivating long-stemmed roses for export to Holland and Germany during the cold European winter. Then as he was easing into middle age the Colonel persuaded him into the Service.

Eliav's curt manner disturbed the Colonel. He knew Eliav hadn't liked his last assignment, but then agents rarely did. They were a breed of men who performed despicable acts because they were necessary, not because they enjoyed doing them. Successful agents were the ones who thought least about where they had been, what they'd done. Most lived for the future, for the next assignment. They were addicts, dependent on the Service as prostitutes are on their pimps; misfits, they find themselves at home nowhere else. But Joseph Eliav was different. He would gladly leave the Service and return to his roses at any time. He stayed simply because he did his job better than anyone else the Colonel could find. And both men knew it.

The Colonel lowered his cup and looked at his old friend. He didn't think the Barth assignment was bothering him. They'd already been over all that, several times. "What's on your mind, Joseph?" he asked, in a soft, sympathetic tone.

Eliav rested both elbows on the table. As he spoke lines of pain pinched his face. "Ari Ben-Sion."

"I see," the Colonel said. He looked out the glass window at an old Arab carrying a pole laden with bunches of bananas. "You know I didn't intend him to die in Syria. He was supposed to escape with the children."

"What difference does that make? You used him when you knew he was too tired to go back in the field. You counted on that, set him up, wanted him to blow everything. You knew there was a good chance he wouldn't come back alive."

"It was a calculated risk. I'd hoped he would survive."

"Damn it. You'd do the same thing to me if it suited your purpose, wouldn't you?"

"Yes," the Colonel said.

Just then a small boy entered the café carrying a tray and darted into the kitchen to fill lunch orders for the shopkeepers in the lanes.

The Colonel sipped his coffee in silence. It was thick and poorly brewed; though he'd drunk only half the cup he could already taste the muddy base. "What about Barth?" he asked, looking up.

"The Russians released him. He's in London."

"How is he?"

"Not good."

The Colonel rubbed the back of his neck. "That could pose a problem. Do you think he's strong enough to return here?"

Eliav nodded. "He should be."

The Colonel pushed his coffee to the side and looked around the room. "What about the Russians? Anybody follow him on the plane?"

"We have to assume someone did. Since 1969 every foreigner who's made contact with a Soviet dissident is followed to the West by a team of KGB agents and the names of the people he goes to see reported to Moscow."

The Colonel slowly withdrew a Dunhill Montecruz cedar-lined aluminum tube from his coat pocket. Unscrewing the cap, he slipped out the cigar. "Unfortunately, the KGB is quite thorough." The Colonel lit his Montecruz and sucked in a mouthful of hot air. "Now, about Barth. I want a twenty-four-hour unseen guard placed on him. And they have to be good men. I don't want the Russians knowing anybody's there."

"All right."

The Colonel pushed the Montecruz tube into his coat pocket. He did not want to leave any trace of his visit in the café.

"What about the KGB agent supposedly operating in London?" Eliav asked. "Have you had any confirmation of his identity?"

"No, not exactly."

"But you are certain there is one?"

The Colonel reached for the cup of coffee he'd pushed aside and spent a long time taking a sip. "I'm rarely certain of anything," he said after setting the cup down.

"You will let me know if you make any progress."

The Colonel nodded.

Eliav didn't believe him. He respected the man, but no longer trusted him. "If we find the KGB's deeply involved in London, that could change everything."

"Yes, it could," the Colonel said.

"The Soviet sleeper agents—we would have to alter our operation."

The Colonel looked up slowly. "I suppose that would be the case."

Eliav pushed his chair back. It was pointless to press the Colonel. He divulged nothing, ever. "Is there anything else?"

"Yes. I was thinking—why don't you go up to the kibbutz for a day or so before you fly back to London? It'll do you some good."

"I'd like that." Eliav rose. "Why don't you join me? We could

127

stop at the wine cellars at Rishon le Zion—pick up some cheese, a bottle of wine, and eat along the beach at Caesarea. I know a great spot, a patch of grass near the Roman wall that's sheltered from the wind. Before Leora died we used to go there often."

The Colonel ground his cigar into a metal ashtray. "I'd love to, Joseph, but I can't." He offered no explanation. Eliav suspected his friend had lost the ability to do anything but work. He nodded and left the café. As he moved through the suq, with the music of Radio Amman wailing from transistor radios, he felt quite sad.

Before leaving the café the Colonel looked around one last time. His associates probably would have been amused had they known he had chosen to meet one of his most deeply placed agents in the midst of the Arab marketplace.

He walked up the incline toward Yafo Gate, his mind busy preparing the path for Barth's return to Israel.

Petr Dmitrivich Grigorenko moved down the green-walled corridor of the Center toward Zavorin's office. In the anteroom the Major General's secretary made him wait nineteen minutes, which quietly added to his anger.

The portrait of Lenin looked down from the wall as Grigorenko stood opposite Zavorin, who, busy outlining his monthly report to the Politburo, did not acknowledge his presence.

"Comrade General."

"Yes, Petr Dmitrivich," Zavorin said without looking up. "What is it you want?"

Standing there, suffering humiliation again, Grigorenko was suddenly sorry he'd demanded to see the First Directorate chief. "An explanation, sir."

"Of what?"

"The Barth business. Why was he released? Why wasn't I informed? The case was under my jurisdiction."

Zavorin dropped his pen on the desk. "I discovered the boy was innocent. Since he had nothing to do with the girl's death, I ordered his expulsion. There was pressure from the American Embassy. I couldn't hold him any longer."

"But why wasn't I consulted?"

"For what reason? The decision was already made."

"But it shouldn't have been made without me," Grigorenko protested. "This was my operation. I infiltrated the Zionist movement."

"You did?" Zavorin said. "That's strange. I thought the Party was responsible for Operation Cloverleaf. My superiors will be very interested, Petr Dmitrivich, to hear you claim the triumph for yourself."

"I do no such thing," Grigorenko said loudly. "You're twisting my words. Nobody will believe you."

"Won't they? Just wait. I have evidence proving that you had Susan Stern murdered to embarrass me. I know what you want. You want to move up from the Fifth Directorate. You want this office?"

The blood left Grigorenko's face. "What are you talking about? "How could you have proof? I had nothing to do with the girl's death."

"You may leave now, Comrade Grigorenko," Zavorin said.

"No, I will not leave until I hear the testimony you have against me."

Zavorin reached for the last of the battery of phones lining the edge of his desk, dialed a one, and asked Yuri Pirozhkov to come in. As he lowered the receiver he turned to Grigorenko. "Do not force me to take stronger measures. Please leave with him."

Grigorenko said nothing. Before the secretary could enter he left the room.

Ten-London

A blaze of light on his eyelids woke Steve. Quickly he sat up in the bed. The covers were tangled and draped half over the floor. The room was cold. Steve remained still, confused about where he was, uncertain if it had happened, if he'd really been to Russia. His first thoughts were that he'd dreamed it all. Often he had trouble remembering if he'd experienced certain events or dreamed them. He looked around the room—the cream-colored walls were bare, the open closet, empty. He remembered now. He was back in London. The same house. He'd taken the bus from the airport, then the underground to Whitechapel. He'd found his way back to this place. Michael, David, and Wulf had been waiting. He told them about Susan, then Michael led him upstairs and gave him a pill.

Steve dropped back on the mattress. His mouth was dry. He closed his eyes and the walls seemed to move inside his head. Though he was cold he didn't bother to cover himself.

What seemed like hours later there was a light tapping on the door and Michael entered the room.

"Are you up?" he asked softly.

Steve lay silent for a moment, then by an act of will pulled himself into a sitting position. "Yes."

"Good. Vicki has some breakfast ready. We thought you might be hungry. Mind you, you slept quite a long time."

"Not long enough," Steve mumbled, reaching for the clothes strewn on the floor.

Downstairs he picked at his eggs and nibbled a thin, heavily buttered slice of white bread.

"I'm not very hungry," he said finally, pushing the food away.

"Do you fancy a cup of tea?" Mike asked.

"All right."

"Some tea, luv," Mike said above the noise of running water.

Vicki put the dish she was washing back in the sink and reached for the kettle of boiling water. She poured the water through a fresh strainer of tea into two cups already a quarter filled with milk. Silently she slipped them onto the table.

Steve brought the hot liquid to his lips. It tasted bitter. There was no sugar on the table. Instead of asking for some, he drank the tea the way it was.

Mike put his cup on the table, not bothering to place it on the saucer. "We can talk now if you're up to it."

"And if I'm not?"

"Then you can relax. Have a walk. We'll talk later."

The prospect of wandering the streets of London, alone, suddenly seemed terrifying. His defiance dissolved. "I'm ready."

Leaving the dishes on the table for Vicki to remove, Michael led the boy into the pine-paneled living room. With the toe of his shoe he touched a switch under the rug, turning on the reel-to-reel tape recorder built into the cabinet behind the television set. He sat on the couch, Steve in the upholstered chair near the bar.

"You met Zev Zaretsky as planned?" Michael asked.

Steve nodded.

"Were you able to deliver the books without interference?"

"Yes."

"Good." Mike moved forward on the couch. "Did he or any of his friends give you a message for us?"

Steve hesitated. "No," he said, after a moment.

Mike registered his hesitation and wondered if the boy was hiding something.

"Are you sure? They must have said something they wanted us to know. Don't answer right away. Think back."

"I am. There was nothing. Most of the time they talked about Hebrew classes, the need for books, how they're harassed by the secret police."

Mike rose and stood over the boy. "Steve, we're in a lot of trouble. All of us. Susan's dead. She's been killed and nobody seems to know why. The only thing we do know is that you're connected to it somehow. You're the link. You're the only one who can provide the answers that will help us out of this mess. Now I'm asking you to cooperate with me. If you do I'll make this as brief and painless as possible. You won't have to talk to anyone else. You can leave here in a day or two. The CIA resident in London has already been around, twice. He wants to take you to Washington and let military intelligence debrief you there. I put him off, told him we were friends, that I'd supply him with a complete report so you wouldn't have to go through this again. I'll only be able to keep him away if I have your full cooperation. Now what were you instructed to tell us?"

Steve shrank back in the chair. He didn't want to tell Mike about Zaretsky's letter, that he'd handed it over without a struggle. There had been so much failure already. He couldn't admit to more.

"I was given no messages," Steve said, rubbing his hands on his pants leg.

The boy's palms must be sweating. He moved closer, leaning lower. "Come on, was it verbal or written?" As he spoke fear flooded the boy's eyes. "I have little patience, Steve. There are plenty of things I'd rather be doing. I can just as easily turn you over to the CIA. They won't take to such stubbornness. They'll have everything out of you in a matter of minutes. But let me warn you, their methods are a bit unpleasant."

Steve said nothing.

"Look, Steve, just tell me and it will be over. You can go home. Forget about all of this."

The boy's eyes were fixed on the floor.

"You went to Zaretsky's apartment, met some of his friends, talked. They asked questions about Israel, you tried to answer them. Then the conversation turned. They asked if you'd be willing to bring some important information to the West. Probably it was written on a sheet of paper. They asked if you thought you could hide it, right? Look at me. Now."

Steve's head came up slowly and looked directly at the man so close above him. His eyes were dark and fierce. Deep lines cut into his face. Yet they hardly moved as he continued talking.

"They didn't pressure you into agreeing to transfer the document. Zaretsky brought it out and put it on the table. He told you about their mail. How they rarely receive it, how all letters sent out of the country are read. He asked if you'd be willing to bring one to us. You agreed. That's how it happened, isn't it?"

"No, it wasn't like that." The words raced out. Steve wanted away from all this. He didn't understand why he'd come back here, to this house. He should have gone back to Israel to . . . "The letter wasn't for you," he blurted. "Zaretsky wanted me to take it to his brother in Mevasseret Zion, the absorption center outside Jerusalem. He hadn't heard from him in four months. He was afraid his letters were being confiscated."

Mike suppressed a smile. Zaretsky was clever. He had tricked the boy, realizing he would agree to act as a courier between two brothers. Zaretsky knew Mike would intercept the letter, meant for him, in London.

His face lost much of its hostility. "Where is the letter now?"

"The KGB's got it. I'm sorry. Susan was keeping it in her purse. I didn't want to have it on her in case we were arrested. While she was in the shower I put the envelope in my pocket. When the Russians arrested me it was there. I couldn't do anything to stop the interrogator. He took it. I should have hidden it better but I . . ."

"So whoever killed her didn't get the letter?"

135

Steve nodded.

Mike moved across the room and settled back on the couch trying to guess what was in the letter, wondering if someone had killed Susan to get a message she no longer possessed. "What about verbal information? Were you asked to tell us anything?"

"Not really."

Mike's mind was racing. He had to keep the boy talking before he reconsidered and demanded to leave. He couldn't hold him in the house against his will. "What about other pieces of evidence: photographs, microfilm. Did they ask you to bring anything like that out?"

"No," Steve said. The image of Andrei's Bible flashed in his mind. Technically he wasn't lying. Mike had said nothing about a book. When the time came Steve would give the Bible to Andrei personally; he wanted that. The young Hebrew teacher had risked a lot coming to the hotel. Andrei's contacting the American Embassy had certainly caused his release.

"Now, about Susan," Mike said. "When did you last see her alive?"

Steve stiffened. "It was in our hotel room." The words caught in his throat. "Yesterday, the day before. I don't remember. Please, I don't know what happened." His voice was harsh, near hysteria. "They asked me that over and over again. Please, I can't go through it again. She told me nothing. I don't know what happened to her. I don't. I don't. You have to believe me. I can't tell you anything." He clawed at the back of his hair. "Why won't you leave me alone?"

As he spoke David moved into the room, walking heavily. He had been listening from the hallway. As he entered he stepped on the switch by the door, shutting off the recording device. He didn't want his voice on tape.

"Vicki, some tea," Mike called into the kitchen as David shuffled his wide frame toward the boy.

"I'm glad you made it back all right," David said, settling deep into the corner of the couch opposite Mike. "Bloody nasty lot, those Russians." He removed a pipe from his jacket pocket, filled it with tobacco, and struck a match. "Sorry they picked you up. Hope they didn't work you over too bad."

"They didn't harm me physically."

David sucked on his pipe. "They rarely do, you know, not with foreigners. Protecting themselves. You'd look silly if you called a press conference complaining about sleeping in a hotel bed and being served three meals a day."

Vicki entered carrying a tray with three cups of milky-brown tea and a plate of English biscuits. Steve took a cup, still not asking for sugar. As she moved toward the other two men it bothered him that she hadn't brought some tea for herself.

David sipped his tea, then balanced the cup and saucer on the arm of the couch. "Steve, I have just a few questions for you. If you answer them, you can leave London tomorrow. If not, I'm afraid you're going to be detained here for quite some time." His voice was soft, sympathetic. "I know you've been through a lot. There's been a balls-up somewhere. Our fault not yours, but there's a possibility you can clear up some unanswered questions. We need your help. Will you give it?"

The boy nodded. Anything to end this.

"Good. Now, the letter Zaretsky requested you deliver to his brother. Did the Russians say anything to you about the contents after they took it from you?"

"No, nothing."

David hadn't thought they would. But it was worth a try. "Steve, we're going to have to talk about Susan for a few minutes. I know the memory is painful, so I'll ask you as few questions as possible. If we do this now, you'll never have to go over it again."

"All right," Steve said. He put his tea on the floor, spilling some of it into the saucer.

"When did you see her last?"

"In the hotel, in the afternoon. The day before yesterday." His voice was flat, emotionless. "We made love. She fell asleep. I went for a walk. When I returned she was gone. There was no note, nothing. She didn't tell me where she was going. She never came back. That night the KGB arrested me."

"Are you sure she didn't hint where she was going, make even a vague reference to who she was meeting? Come on, Steve, she must have said something."

"She didn't," he shouted, suddenly wild with rage. It was the same thing. He couldn't take it. "You used me, both of you. Told me Susan would come along so I wouldn't look suspicious, a college student traveling alone. You lied to me. I know she was a CIA agent. The Russians told me." Again he approached hysteria. "Why'd you do it? Why did you send her?"

"All right," David said. The tone of authority in his voice was intimidating. "If you want the truth, you'll have it. She was sent for your protection. We felt there was a possibility you might be picked up and interrogated. As long as the girl was around and you'd have to face her we assumed your pride would prevent you from breaking. She served as our safety measure."

What? The blood pushed hotly against Steve's cheeks. Though he didn't like the idea, he saw that they were right; his ego probably would have sanctioned his silence. They had manipulated him for his own good.

David kept talking. He didn't want the boy to have a chance to stop and analyze the situation. "About Zaretsky's letter. Do you think Susan knew you took it?"

"No. I don't know." He fell back in the chair. "She didn't say." The letter again. The Russians had said nothing about it. Why were they so interested in the letter?

David's pipe went out. He took a lighter off the coffee table, held the gas flame across the bowl, sucking in, and let the smoke drift along the edges of his mouth.

"Do you think it's possible," David began, "that someone killed Susan in order to get Zaretsky's letter?"

"But that doesn't make sense. She didn't have it on her. I did."

"The assailant wouldn't have known that. Susan may have thought she still had it."

Steve pulled a handkerchief from his pocket. "Why would anyone have killed her? Even to get the letter. He could have taken it and let her go."

There was a long silence, the only sound that of dishes being put away in the kitchen.

Finally Mike spoke. "She may have recognized him."

Steve sat, the damp handkerchief clenched in his hands. He said nothing. His eyes were glassy, swollen.

"What do you want to do, Steve?" Michael asked.

"I don't know."

"Is there anyone you'd like us to contact, talk to for you?"

He shook his head.

Mike paused, then continued. "Steve, I want you to know

that even though everything didn't work out as planned, you may have helped us quite a bit."

What did it matter? He said nothing. *Everything didn't work out as planned.* The phrase repeated itself in his mind. Such a cheapening of life—not just Susan's life. All life.

"We have a ticket for you," David said. "Back to Israel. It's in the desk drawer by your bed along with an El Al flight schedule. You can make a reservation by phone whenever you like. Let us know and Mike will run you to the airport."

Steve rose slowly. He didn't know where he would go, and he didn't care. He looked at the two men. The words he wanted came easily.

"I'll take the underground."

Piccadilly Circus. An explosion of traffic and people. Posters, T-shirts, souvenir shops, postcard stands, ice cream vendors. At the Classic Theatre: FRAULEINS IN UNIFORM; THE RAPE. Across the roundabout: BOOTS DISPENSING CHEMISTS; WARD'S IRISH HOUSE.

Joseph Eliav edged through the throng into Lower Regent Street, his eye catching the column crowned with the statue of Frederick, Duke of York, commander-in-chief of the British Army from 1795 to 1827. Crossing at the signal, he entered the Ceylon Tea Centre, pausing to study the walls adorned with pictures of the Hindu temple at Trincomalee.

The American, Phillip F eske, would be waiting in the Kandy Tea Bar, downstairs. Furious, he'd demanded an immediate meeting. Eliav didn't blame him. Situations reversed, he'd be rather angry himself. Nobody likes to lose an agent—that is, unless they order the elimination themselves.

Chest-high tables filled the basement room. Harried travelers could stand at them, eat, and gulp their tea free from the demands of people or patience. Along the walls were small square tables, chairs facing center. From them one could observe everything in the room.

Phillip Fleske was sitting in the far corner. Eliav went to the cafeteria-style counter, took a cup of strong Uva tea and a cream-filled cake, and joined the American.

Fleske, a Psychological Warfare and Paramilitary staff officer with the Clandestine Services division of the CIA, liaison link to MI-5 in London, wore a three-piece business suit, the vest tight on his stocky frame. Eliav tried to read, unsuccessfully, whatever message Fleske's eyes might convey. His brown-tinted glasses concealed everything but tiredness.

"I cancelled two appointments and came as soon as I could," Eliav said, wanting Fleske to feel important. It was the best way to deal with Americans. They were hard to handle when they lost status.

Fleske coughed, a hard, racking whine. He brought his fist to his mouth, trying to smother the sound. But he couldn't. His whole body was shaking. Curious, people turned their heads, then, quickly bored, returned to their business. Eliav waited until the coughing subsided. "Damn dampness," Fleske muttered.

"From the Midwest, aren't you?"

"Kansas," he said. "You?"

"You mean originally?"

Fleske nodded.

"I was born in Donetsk, a mining city in the Ukraine." Eliav decided not to lie. Keeping to the truth whenever possible made his cover real, his past less suspicious.

Fleske held his cup to his lips. The coffee was lukewarm and bitter. It left an unpleasant taste, but he drank it anyway, slowly. The coughing had broken the edge off his anger; he wanted time to regain it. The President, equally incensed, was intending to lodge an official protest over what had happened in Moscow. But before he acted there were certain details he demanded to be clarified. "Who killed the girl?" Fleske asked.

"I don't know," Eliav said. "I suppose it was the Russians."

"Come on, you don't bloody believe that. Too obvious. Not KGB style, killing agents in their front yard."

"If they had a reason, they would kill her."

Fleske removed his glasses and rubbed his forehead with the balls of his palm. "Okay, granted. But it would have to be a damn good reason. None of this carrying Hebrew books shit." He struck the table with his fist, rattling the silverware. "I don't understand what the hell happened. You asked me to provide an agent to act as companion to your boy, someone who'd watch over him, who he could talk to if he got scared. That's all. She wasn't supposed to do anything and she wasn't supposed to get killed!"

Eliav searched the American's eyes. They were small and red, worn by the agony of insomnia. They testified to a will that might break under excessive pressure. Eliav would move gently. Though the distinction was often minimal, this was an ally not an adversary.

"It's possible," Eliav suggested, "that the girl learned something that rendered her a danger to the Russians. If that was the case, they would have had no choice but to silence her."

"But why her and not the boy?"

"She was an agent, he only an amateur."

"They couldn't have known that," Fleske said. "She was new,

unknown behind the Iron Curtain, her cover impenetrable."

"Agreed . . . unless the Russians were tipped off. Which, I believe, is what happened."

Fleske swore under his breath, realizing suddenly where Eliav was headed. "They've placed an agent among our British associates."

"I would say that is our only conclusion."

"Do you know who it is?"

"No," Eliav said. "That's why I thought it best we talk before Michael Marks joins us."

Fleske reached into his inner coat pocket and withdrew a soft pack of the Camel cigarettes he got duty-free through the embassy. He tapped the filterless cigarette against the table, then lit it. The hot smoke burned his lungs and he coughed. "I'll get my people on this thing right away. The Deputy Director of Plans should be most interested, not to mention MI-5 and the Special Branch. Any help you can give us will be appreciated."

"I'll pass that on to the Colonel. I'm sure he'll want to cooperate."

Fleske tasted the roundness of the cigarette, aware that his anger had seeped away. Though a part of him wished to regain its power, another part was too exhausted to bother. Really, agents were killed all the time. What difference did the loss of the girl make? Besides, she was Jewish. Like Michael, Wulf, and David, she showed evidence of a divided loyalty, a dual allegiance to the United States and to Israel. Fleske surrendered to the ease of indifference. "What could they have stumbled onto, the two of them?" he asked. "We have to assume if the Russians killed Susan that it was something important."

Eliav nodded.

"In all likelihood they were given some documents or messages to bring out," Fleske said.

"Marks did mention a letter."

"That could be it. What did he say?"

"Not much. We spoke on the phone. He agreed to meet us here." Eliav checked his watch. "He's due any moment."

Fleske grunted, then sat in silence eyeing the untouched slice of cake beside Eliav's cup. He was trying to watch his weight, drop a few pounds. But the more effort he expended at curbing his appetite, the more he ate.

Eliav followed his eyes. "Would you like half?" he offered, pushing the small plate across the table. "Don't know why I got it in the first place. I'm not very hungry."

"No thanks."

"Come on, try a piece. Fantastic sweets they have here. If you don't take some, the whole thing will wind up in the rubbish."

"All right," Fleske said, digging a fork into the end of the chocolate cream cake. "You talked me into it."

As the American quickly chewed the food, Eliav smiled. "Go on, finish it."

Fleske lowered his head. "If you're going to throw it away . . ." He moved the plate nearer.

Eliav sipped his tea in satisfaction. Watching Fleske devour the cake he knew he'd achieved some small advantage over his ally.

"By the way," the Israeli said as Fleske lit another cigarette, "have you made much progress in uncovering the Russians' new communications network?"

Fleske sucked on the cigarette, coughing up the smoke. "A little. We're fairly certain they're using microdots. Don't know where they're hiding them." The coughing pounded at his chest again. Reluctantly he ground out his cigarette. "Do know they're using agents posing as Jewish immigrants for couriers. Damned impossible to ferret them out, not to mention identifying the clean ones sent as sleepers. Over a hundred thousand of your people have come out of Russia since the 'sixty-seven war. Now half of them are going to the United States. It's an impossible task trying to watch all of them . . . for years."

"That's why it's crucial we break the KGB's new communications network. The couriers will ultimately lead us to the sleepers. The process is inevitable. The Colonel believes priority must be established there. We must identify those sleepers. Once they are drafted and work their way up our army ranks there's no telling what they'll learn and pass on to Moscow. The only thing certain is that they'll have access to the most sophisticated and secret American military equipment."

"I know," Fleske said.

Just then Michael Marks moved down the staircase into the tea bar. He proceeded to the counter and ordered a pot of Nuwara Eliya, a light blend of Ceylon tea.

"How's the boy?" Fleske asked when Marks joined them.

"He's shaken, a bit incoherent, but physically unharmed."

"And psychologically?" Eliav asked.

"Unstable. I think he fell for the girl. That didn't help any."

"It never does," Fleske said under his breath.

"What about Barth's plans?" Eliav asked. "Did he take the return ticket to Israel?"

"Yes. I assume he'll use it. Don't think he'll want to hang around here very long." Mike poured half the contents of the metal pot into his cup. He liked the rest of his tea to remain as hot as possible. "But I don't understand. Why are you so anxious that he return to Israel? You want your boys to have a go at him?"

"No, there's no need to put him through all that. But the Colonel's worried," Eliav lied. "He thinks the boy may know something the Russians will soon want. If they come after him, we'll be in a better position to protect him in Jerusalem."

"I see," Michael said. Eliav's explanation struck him as vague. Though Marks didn't believe him, he was pleased that Barth would soon be removed from his responsibility, regardless of the reason. He didn't like this whole business, dealing with kids.

"I understand he had a letter on him," Fleske said.

"Yes. The Russians confiscated it during the interrogation."

"You have any idea what was in the letter?"

"The boy said Zaretsky gave it to him to deliver to his brother in Israel. I doubt that was the case. Zaretsky probably wanted to tell us something and coded it in the letter, knowing we would read it before allowing the message to continue to Jerusalem. This of course brings up the possibility that the KGB killed Susan to get the letter. She was carrying it up until the last minute when Barth took it from her."

"What a mess," Fleske said in frustration. "We better get to Zaretsky right away and find out what the hell the Russians know that we don't."

"I agree," Eliav said.

Michael took a long drink from his cup. "I'll get on it immediately. But it'll take time to book a tour. The Moscow Intourist hotels are jammed in the summer. I don't think I'll be able to get anybody inside for at least two weeks."

"Do the best you can," Eliav said.

Marks nodded.

"How's the wife and kids?" Eliav asked after a long pause, feeling the business at hand was all but completed.

"Vicki's fine. I've got the boys at Wulf's until this business blows over and Barth's gone. They pick up too much around the house, even at their age."

"And David?"

"The same. He's got himself a new young bird and a police van. For the life of me I don't understand how he gets ahold of either."

Eliav laughed lightly.

"How about you, Joseph? Any chance you and Millie getting serious? I like weddings. I haven't been to a good do in ages."

Fleske leaned back in his chair detached, distant. He distrusted these Jews, the bond they all seemed to feel with each other. He didn't understand how Wulf, Marks, and David had built an independent intelligence service with operatives in every country in Europe. Couldn't figure out how they'd managed it without resources and the backing of a sovereign nation. Just because most of them were kids during the war and too young to fight Hitler didn't seem to be reason enough to exhaust their time and personal incomes the way they did. It was unnatural. Some of them, cab drivers, could hardly pay their bills because they practically lived at the airport photographing the continual arrival and departure of Russians and Arabs. He didn't understand Jews, didn't like their obsession with the past. Why did they think they were so special? A lot of people had died in the war.

He scraped the bottom of the plate for cake crumbs, dropped the fork on the table, then excused himself and left.

*   *   *

Petr Dmitrivich Grigorenko, traveling on a forged Finnish passport, cleared customs at Heathrow Airport with minimal delay. He was in a hurry. Having left Moscow without Zavorin's knowledge, he wanted to return as soon as possible, before his absence was noticed. Consequently he'd taken a direct Aeroflot flight instead of traveling to Helsinki and switching to Finnair.

Wulf stood leaning against the currency exchange booth at Heathrow watching passengers stride through the green "Nothing to Declare" line. He was part of a two-man team. Darryl, up close, photographed each arriving passenger with his Minox, while he stood back attempting to spot anyone of particular interest. Wulf studied the photographs nightly, knew the regulars, the trade mission people—hardly had to glance at them. If nothing better turned up, he'd lure one of them into his cab and put his luggage and briefcases up front in the empty space near the driver's seat, to be rifled as he sped toward the West End. Occasionally he'd spot somebody special. He had the picture of every known KGB agent tucked in his memory. Several times a year somebody he recognized came through—and that made all the waiting worthwhile.

When Wulf saw Colonel Petr Grigorenko, head of the Jewish Department of the Fifth Chief Directorate, walking quickly toward the exit he stood still, too excited to move. Grigorenko, the man directly responsible for the crackdown on the Jewish dissidents, for the closing of the *Chronicle of Current Events*—Wulf couldn't believe he was here, so close, within reach. His emotions seized control. He would maneuver the Russian behind the terminal, grab him around the neck, squeeze . . .

Quickly he calmed himself. This was too crucial an opportunity to spoil with sentiment. Grigorenko would not venture to London for a holiday; he was here to contact someone. Wulf moved across the small expanse between them, cutting in front of other passengers, reaching the Russian.

"Cab, sir?" he asked. Before Grigorenko could respond Wulf took the small valise from his hand. "Let me 'ave your bag. My cab's right around the side. Takes forever, waiting in the rank. It's a bit dicey, but everybody's got to make a living, right, mate?"

Grigorenko nodded, his thoughts on the meeting he was about to initiate and the danger.

"Where to?" Wulf asked as they reached the big black Austin cab.

"Just drive until you see a call box."

"I'll 'ave you at one straightaway, sir."

Wulf jumped into the cab and threw the heavy vehicle in gear. Leaving the airport, he headed north on Sipson Road toward the M4 Motorway. Before the junction he stopped at a red, glass-enclosed telephone booth across from the Hollycroft post office. As Grigorenko reached in his pocket for a two-pence coin and jumped out to make his call, Wulf switched off the ignition. A few minutes later the Russian returned and walked around the cab to the driver's side. "Take me to the Tate Gallery."

"Consider yourself there," Wulf said.

As the cab sped toward the West End, Grigorenko shut his eyes and tried to rest. He didn't like being in the capitalist world; he preferred not seeing it. For what he was told and what he saw differed so radically that there was no reconciliation. And he didn't dare question what he was told. That would have paralyzed him, made him unable to go on with his work. If he relinquished his work, there would be nothing left in his life. Nothing.

The Tate Gallery overlooks Lambeth Bridge and the muddy Thames. Wulf pulled up in front of the structure, built in the free classical style of the 1890s, and let his passenger out. Grigorenko moved up the stone steps. Wulf pulled to the corner as if looking for a fare and waited. A few minutes later he saw something that accelerated his heartbeat and dampened the shirt near his armpits. His governor, David, appeared from around the far corner near the Queen's Military Hospital and slowly mounted the entrance steps to the gallery, pushing his fat frame up each one with conscious effort.

Wulf trounced on the accelerator and turned up Atterbury Street, narrowly missing a green Vauxhall that had to slam on the brakes to avoid hitting him. Panic, anger, and fear collided inside him in a kaleidoscope of despair. There had been rumors for months, unsubstantiated, that their organization had been infiltrated, that information was being channeled to the KGB. Repeated attempts to investigate each link in the chain of command had turned up nothing. Here, by accident, he'd discovered the break. At the top. David. And it had been David who'd first suggested they send a young American to Moscow. That meant the Russians were behind Barth's trip. He had to tell somebody. But who? How far did the deception descend? He had to go to somebody neutral, someone on the outside. He made a sharp right up Islip Street, tires screeching. He'd go to the American, Phillip Fleske.

Grigorenko proceeded to Gallery 8, as David had advised, surprised and a bit disturbed not to find him waiting there. Impatiently Grigorenko ran his eyes from one painting to the next: J.M.W. Turner, works painted during two visits to Italy made by the artist in 1819 and 1828. They bored him, *Venus Reclining* and *Southern Landscape with Aqueduct and Waterfall.* He couldn't understand what prompted people to spend hours wandering around places like this.

Minutes later David moved into the room, pleased that the gallery was quiet. Grigorenko turned from *The Bay of Baiae.*

"I'm glad you could come," he said as the fat man neared.

"A call from you is, shall I say, unexpected."

"I came to London specifically so we could talk."

David's face registered none of the surprise he felt. The layers of his cheeks remained motionless, his eyes deceptively dull. Grigorenko had initiated the meeting; he would wait to find out why.

"I believe we might be able to work together for our mutual benefit," Grigorenko said.

"Go on."

"I need an ally, a partner to unite with me against a common enemy."

"We have a common enemy?"

"I think we do . . . in Alexandr Mikhailovich Zavorin."

David waited for a long moment before responding. He was beginning to understand. The tug for power at the top, the same everywhere, unending; as soon as one of the combatants was pulled to the dirt, another rose to take up the challenge. "And you think I can help you?"

"Yes."

"What will I receive in return?"

"I am privy to much information I think you'd find of interest. If I succeed I would not be unwilling to share it with you." Grigorenko paused purposefully. "And then there is the possibility that the Fifth Chief Directorate will need a new director."

Just then a uniformed guard entered the room and studied the two men for a moment. Satisfied that they had no intention of mutilating the paintings, he continued into Gallery 7.

"You realize you're taking quite a risk exposing yourself to me," David said. "What if I should contact Zavorin and offer to trade the particulars of this discussion for a promotion to Moscow?"

"The knowledge I have about a KGB agent directing the Zionists in London should insure my safety. If that information reached certain parties, you'd be dead within the hour." But behind Grigorenko's words his face paled.

David allowed a smile to show on his lips. "I think our association could be of mutual benefit," he said. "What do you want me to do?"

Grigorenko looked around the gallery again, assuring himself that no one was listening. "Zavorin, as you know, is violently opposed to detente with the Americans. His personal opinion in this area is widely acknowledged, but he remains in power because he keeps his views private. Publicly he's gone along with Brezhnev at every turn; but there are those on the Politburo who believe he is biding time, waiting for a chance to strike at the Americans and weaken detente. When the attack comes it's expected to be launched in such a way that no one will realize Zavorin is the perpetrator."

"Of course. If it were known Zavorin damaged detente against Party wishes, Brezhnev would destroy him."

"My conclusion exactly. That's why when the time comes I want you to verify the report I intend to make stating Zavorin ordered you to approach the London CIA resident, Phillip Fleske, and persuade him to send one of his young female operatives into Russia with Steven Barth. I want it to look like Zavorin brought the girl to Russia."

David moved toward the entrance to Gallery 9. From the doorway he could see some of Turner's small Italian landscapes and he looked at the *Coast Scene*, near Naples, reviewing the conspirator's words in his mind. Assuming that the backlash from the murder of a young girl would weaken relations with the United States, Grigorenko would make it look like Zavorin sent Susan to Russia with the singular purpose of killing her. At the proper time Grigorenko would expose Zavorin's unauthorized blow at detente and depose him. Grigorenko could pull it off. Murdering the girl to strike at detente was an act all believed Zavorin capable of committing.

The Fifth Directorate officer followed David to the doorway. He moved close. "Do I have your cooperation?"

David waited a long moment, his eyes following the paintings. "Yes," he said finally.

"Good. Then if you'll excuse me I have a plane to catch. I want to return to Moscow as soon as possible, before I'm missed."

"Of course."

David watched him leave the museum, hurrying too quickly. That was a mistake; it would attract attention. Clearly, Grigorenko was inexperienced in the field.

After moving through the rest of the Turner collection David entered Gallery 13, housing the English Impressionists, Steer and Sickert. He had done the right thing, agreeing to join Grigorenko. Actually, he would stay neutral, monitor each side, promote both, then in the end declare allegiance with the victor.

After a sufficient amount of time had passed David shuffled toward the exit. He would have to proceed cautiously. Grigorenko was as ruthless as he was ambitious. Apparently he'd killed Susan so he could blame her death on Zavorin.

Alexandr Mikhailovich Zavorin sat at his desk, a photocopy of Zaretsky's letter flat on the mahogany surface before him. He stared at it, hands on his knees. There was something there, had to be. But what? He poured a cup of lukewarm tea from the samovar behind him, spilled some of the contents into the saucer, and brought it to his lips with both hands. He'd puzzled over the series of sentences for two days now, without success. The letter *seemed* innocuous: Zaretsky telling his brother about the most recent persecutions, his desire to leave for Israel, the anti-Semitic taunting his daughter Katia endured at school, the report he'd received about the desecration of a Jewish cemetery in Odessa, and a special hello to their dear friends Margalit Poe and Boris Begun.

Zavorin rose and moved to the window to meditate. Drawing back the heavy silk curtains, he watched the trolley buses move from Kirov Street, circle the worn brown granite, flower-planted island surrounding the statue of Felix Dzerzhinsky, and pass directly under his window. His thoughts followed the bus out of sight and returned to the letter. At first he had thought Odessa was the key word, suspecting that the name of the city referred to the ODESSA, the Organisation der SS-Angehörigen—Organization of SS members. But upon checking he discovered that a cemetery in the old Jewish quarter of the city of Odessa had recently been plowed to make room for a housing project. So he abandoned that tack and ordered the original letter swept for invisible ink, microdots, and a hidden layer of paper—all to no avail. As a last resort he suggested the text be translated into Yiddish and Hebrew, hoping something might turn up when the words were transposed. He was still waiting for a report from his language experts.

Meanwhile he refilled his saucer and allowed his thoughts to turn to Comrade Grigorenko. The head of the Fifth Chief Directorate's Jewish Department had flown to London on an unscheduled trip. Zavorin wanted to know why. Unfortunately he'd not learned of Grigorenko's plans early enough to send anyone to follow him. But that oversight could be countered. He made a mental note to contact David in London and find out what Grigorenko had been doing there.

Soon the characteristic three short taps of Zavorin's secretary echoed through the large room.

"Enter," he said, returning to his overstuffed chair.

Yuri Pirozhkov moved into the room, closing the door behind him. "The language department has found something, Alexandr Mikhailovich." He always addressed the First Directorate head by his familiar name and patronymic when they were alone. "They are not certain of the reference but it may mean something to you."

"Go on."

"It was in one of the names, a hidden Hebrew phrase. Let me show you." He took out a thick card with two lines of writing on it, identical except the first word was slightly longer than the one beneath it.

מרגלי' פה

מרגל פה

"The top one," Pirozhkov continued, "is a name, Margalit Poe. You remember in the letter Zaretsky said a special hello to his friends Margalit Poe and Boris Begun."

Zavorin nodded.

"The second word is Hebrew for *spy here*."

A smile broke over Zavorin's face.

Pirozhkov realized he'd delivered the news Alexandr Mikhailovich required. He waited, knowing Zavorin would want to savor his victory before responding with further orders.

The pleasure invading Zavorin's mind faded quickly. Having discovered somehow that a spy had infiltrated the Jewish dissidents in Moscow, Zaretsky was attempting to deliver that information to the West. He had to be stopped, immediately, before another courier was sent to contact him and the information transferred. If the agent was compromised, the plan to activate the sleepers, using Barth, would be in jeopardy.

"You are familiar with the Zionist Zev Zaretsky?" Zavorin asked, looking up at his secretary.

"Yes."

"I want him called for reserve military duty today and stationed near the Chinese border, at Arkhara. Pick him up without notice. Don't let him speak to anyone, even for a moment. Then call General Oleg Lyudin in Arkhara. Tell him Zaretsky's being flown in by special plane." Zavorin leaned back in his chair, pushing his desk drawer closed with his foot. "Oleg's an old friend. You might mention that I would be in his debt if the Jew should happen to be killed by a stray bullet during a training exercise."

"It will be taken care of immediately."

As his secretary left, Zavorin turned toward the windows and played the last day's events over in his head. He was searching for any contingency he had not anticipated. Finding none, he allowed his mind to rest. Though no operation was without flaws, he believed himself fully prepared for the unexpected.

The El Al Boeing 707-320C lifted sluggishly off the runway at Heathrow and climbed over the patchwork fields of Kent. Past the cliffs of Dover the sea below seemed deep and distant, shimmering as the sun's rays swept its surface. Ahead stretched the vast expanse of France. Four and a half hours would take the plane to Tel Aviv, twenty-eight thousand feet at a cruising speed of six hundred miles an hour, hurtling across the belly of Europe, the Yugoslavian coastline, the open Mediterranean, before descent and the shoreline of Israel.

Steve sat slumped by the window, his head dug into the small pillow. On the open tray before him rested the remains of three gin and tonics. He hadn't let the stewardess remove the plastic cups. Chewing the ice gave him something to do. He didn't like the taste of hard liquor and had selected gin as the least unpalatable alternative, hoping the alcohol would help him sleep. It hadn't worked.

Upon landing in Tel Aviv he felt no sense of relief, no comfort associated with returning home. He felt nothing. He cleared the requisite document inspection stations, slung his backpack over his shoulder, and headed toward the *sheirut*, shared taxi, station.

The driver took his luggage, ushered him into the back of an old black nine-passenger Mercedes, then hurried toward the terminal in search of additional passengers. Soon the vehicle, fully loaded, moved through the humid summer heat toward the security checkpoint just before the Petah Tikvah-Ramla highway. Steve leaned against the seat, his damp shirt sticking to the vinyl upholstery.

The taxi sped through the Ramla junction and veered left to take the faster road, bypassing the Arab village of Abu Gosh. On both sides of the highway, kibbutz groves, edged by cypresses protecting the fruit from the stiff winds, gave way to pines that soared abruptly up the rocky terrain. From the Bab el Wad, the Gate of the Valley, the car entered a narrow gorge and for twenty-five miles the ribbon of concrete climbed and twisted through the forest, cresting two thousand feet above the coastal plain. Once in Jerusalem, the *sheirut* raced down Yafo Road and slammed to a halt at its home office on Luntz Street just before Zion Square.

Steve took his pack from the trunk and lifted it onto his back. He trudged along Yafo Road toward the small apartment he rented on the outskirts of Mahane Yehuda, a quarter of the inner city known for its outdoor food market and inexpensive housing.

In a narrow alley a group of ragged schoolboys were playing soccer with a flat, patched ball. Steve pushed past them, through a squeaky iron gate into a stone courtyard. He descended four steps below street level to the chained iron door sealing his basement apartment. He inserted a key into the lock, let the chain fall noisily against the stone step, and thrust his way inside. The large, cavelike room was dark, musky, and cold; the small window high above his bed was shut. He lowered his pack to the floor and stood there flooded with an overwhelming sense of loss and loneliness.

He wanted to scream, pound at the walls with his fists, but he didn't move or utter a sound.

Crossing the low-ceilinged room, he lay on the bed and squeezed his eyes shut. His thoughts drifted off the edge of consciousness, falling ... falling. ...

Eleven-Vienna

With the grating of metal against metal the blue and yellow TU 2 locomotive pulling the Chopin Express screeched into the Süd-bahnhof station at seven-nineteen A.M. The journey from Moscow had taken thirty-one hours and four minutes; the train was only nine minutes late.

As the gray-uniformed Bundes Gendarmerie hurried off the platform and out of the station Austrian policemen, clutching short-muzzled Walther MPL submachine guns, surrounded Track 2. Since the hijacking of the train by Arab terrorists in 1973, security had been tight.

Jewish Agency personnel and the usual baggage carriers moved toward the passenger car attempting to separate emigrants from other travelers. This time the Russians had allowed fourteen Jews to board the train and ride to new lives in the West. It was not an unusually large number. About thirty Jews were currently arriving in Vienna each day; but since this was the first of the three trains and two planes that brought the emigrants, it was a promising start.

The Jews were quickly ushered across the outdoor platform and guided into two vans, their motors already idling. In front and behind them, white VW police cars, the blue roof lights rotating, stood ready to escort the caravan out of the station. Minutes later a uniformed officer, standing alone alongside Track 7, gave a signal and the vehicles moved out.

Twelve miles east of the city stretched Schwechat Airport, the final destination in Austria of those Jews choosing to continue to Israel. Their passage through Vienna would be brief. The emigrants had to be processed within seventy-two hours, then transferred to El Al jets, following the unfailing logic that the quicker the Jews were out of the country, the less chance terrorists would have to kill them. The new processing camp, established after Austrian Chancellor Kreisky capitulated to the terrorists in 1973 and closed the transit camp at Schoenau Castle, was a Red Cross station situated a short distance from the airport.

The vans proceeded along a winding road through tree-lined suburbs, the passengers inside atypically quiet. Stunned, excited, afraid, they looked through the windows, trying to peer into the corridor of freedom separating them from the past. Though they came from different cities and villages and had left for many reasons, some dreaming of the land of Israel, others only of escaping Soviet tyranny, they shared a common history, a common destiny.

Soon the caravan entered a high-walled, barbed-wire-encircled compound ringed on the outside by six- and seven-story apartment buildings. Ushered by armed Austrian soldiers into a small single-story building, isolated from the rest of the camp for security reasons, they stood close together as El Al personnel carried their luggage in from the vans. Later all articles brought out of Russia would be carefully scrutinized by Mossad intelligence agents, but for now the suitcases and boxes were placed on long, low tables and each emigrant was required to identify and open his. Still silent, the Jews complied. As the shirt-sleeved security team rifled through the bags in search of guns and explosives, the stench of spoiled food struck the air. From boxes, suitcases, and trunks they removed greasy sausages, sweating cheese, and rotting fish, wrapped in days-old issues of *Pravda* and *Izvestia*. A large trashcan was hauled into the room and the food thrown inside. The Jews looked at each other embarrassed. Unsure of what to expect in the West, they had not wanted to go hungry. They were led back outside, Andrei Bukharov among them.

After a general orientation meeting covering procedure for the next seventy-two hours, information about absorption and language instruction in Israel, and a short question-and-answer period, the emigrants were assigned temporary housing and taken to the central cafeteria for a kosher meal, the first most of them had ever eaten. Since they had to leave Austria within three days, they would be allowed only a few minutes' rest before individual interviews began.

*　　*　　*

The transit camp director, Monek Stark, sat in his office waiting for the next immigrant to be brought in. Behind Stark's cluttered desk was a faded Hebrew map of Europe, its edges yellow and cracked. Across from him, above a threadbare couch, was a large black and white picture of bodies being shoveled out of the ovens at Buchenwald, where Stark had been interned for three years. He had interviewed eleven of the new arrivals so far. With only three more to go he was anxious to complete the work as soon as possible. A plane and second train were due from Moscow in less than an hour.

As Andrei Bukharov entered and seated himself in the hard wood chair facing the desk, the station director gazed out the window. He could see the upper floors of the apartment buildings across the street that protruded above the barbed-wire wall encircling the compound. Though Israeli security teams had taken up permanent residence in each of the buildings, their proximity still worried him. If an Arab suicide squad managed to smuggle one of the new 82mm M-37 mortars they'd recently received from the Russians into a top apartment, they would be able to destroy much of the transit station—almost effortlessly.

"Name?" Stark asked, pen in hand, turning his attention to the young man.

"Andrei Bukharov."

"Place of birth and date?"

"I was born on June 12, 1950 in Moscow."

"Father's name and patronymic?"

"Alexi Vasilevich."

"Father's nationality?"

"Russian."

"Mother's given and maiden name?"

"Larissa Polsky."

"Mother's nationality?"

"*Yevrey*. My mother was Jewish. She raised me by herself. My father died when I was a child. I'm told he was a devout atheist."

"I didn't know there was any other kind." A smile spread up Stark's face. "Let me see your travel document, Andrei."

Andrei removed the pinkish sheet, folded into three parts, and pushed it across the desk. Stark took it, searching first for sweaty fingerprints, a sign that the boy was nervous. He felt none. Glancing quickly at the Dutch and Austrian visas on pages two and three (Holland serving as Israel's representative in the Soviet Union in the absence of diplomatic relations) he returned to the front flap and found the information he wanted.

"I see you are registered as Russian," Stark said.

"My father demanded it."

The camp commander swore to himself. These were the hardest cases to verify. Parents of differing nationalities could choose to register their offspring under either nationality. Hoping to spare their children the burden of prejudice, often even devout Jews listed their sons and daughters as Russians.

"Were you baptized?" Stark continued, pen poised to transfer the response to the sheet before him.

"No."

Stark checked the appropriate box. "What languages do you speak?"

"Russian, some English, and Hebrew."

"Hebrew." The transit station director looked up. Very few of the immigrants had even heard of Yom Kippur; one who spoke

Hebrew was all the more rare. "How did you learn the language?" he asked.

"From textbooks and tapes brought to Moscow by American tourists. Zev Zaretsky and Fayim Orlov, two friends, and I studied the books at night, together. We tutored each other. It didn't take long for us to learn enough to be able to help others begin to study."

Stark's expression remained unchanged. He had other questions to ask, other immigrants to interview. He wrote HEBREW TEACHER in large letters on Bukharov's sheet and moved his mind to the next question. He'd let the boys in Tel Aviv figure out what to do with this one. His job was to provide them with preliminary information, nothing more.

"How long did you wait for your visa?" Stark went on.

"A year and a half. I was turned down once. I waited twelve months, then applied again."

"Where was your last place of employment?"

"I was trained at the Lebedev Institute of Physics of the Academy of Sciences. I was still a student there when I first applied for a visa. Upon receiving my Candidate's Degree the only work I could find was as a baker's loader."

"Name and last place of employment," Stark repeated.

"Bakery Number Fifteen on Malay Gruzinskaya Street," Andrei said, pausing a long moment before speaking. He was never in a hurry.

"May I have the address and occupation of your mother?"

"My mother's dead," he said, emotion soft in his voice.

"Do you have any relatives in Israel?"

"No."

"The name and address of your closest living relative?"

"I have an uncle, Boris Bukharov. He lives in Rostov-on-Don. I'm sorry I don't remember the address."

Stark looked at Bukharov. He appeared calm, relaxed. He was young and he already spoke the language. The boy would adjust easily to Israel.

"Thank you very much, Andrei. We'll try and have you on a plane to Tel Aviv late tomorrow."

"I'd like to go out as soon as possible." His words carried excitement. "I've been waiting a long time."

"Be patient for a few more hours. You're almost there."

"I know, but it's hard when I'm so close." Andrei smiled, shook his outstretched hand, and left the room.

Stark leaned back in his chair and sipped from a glass of water. Turning toward the phone, he dialed a one and his assistant, Isser Infeld, came into the room.

"Are you ready for the Alexandrovichs?" Infeld asked.

Stark set the water on top of a two-day-old still unread edition of the *Kurier*. "Give me a few seconds."

"What about the last one?" Infeld asked.

"Bukharov? There's a tough, determined personality. That boy learned and taught Hebrew in the underground despite the risks. I'm partial to the type. Wish we had more like him. Too many coming through lately just want to get out of Russia—they couldn't care less about Israel."

"I know. They seem to be hitching a free ride at our expense."

"You better get the next ones," Stark said abruptly. "I don't want to start running late."

Infeld stepped into the hall to get Leonid and Sylva Alexandrovich.

The information gathered on each Russian immigrant was fed into a giant Cyber 76 computer housed in an underground complex below Ramat Gan outside Tel Aviv. There the Mossad stored the history of every Russian Jew living in the West. As a further security measure all new immigrants were watched for five years. Every twelve months a report providing information about their friends, contacts, and activities was punched into the computer and correlated against known KGB activity. At best this was a feeble attempt to isolate and identify those Soviet spies posing as Jews. The tiny state lacked the manpower for the adequate surveillance of the nearly 100,000 Russian immigrants absorbed into all branches of the Israeli economy and military.

The responsibility for the security of the state rested with the Colonel. And Stark knew, as did the head of the Israeli Secret Service, that the most they could hope for was to identify a tiny fraction of the hundreds of Soviet agents who had made their way to Israel, Europe, and the United States.

Twelve-Jerusalem

Steve heard the heavy door to his apartment open and he looked up as Dahlia entered. Shorts and a low-cut white blouse revealed smooth olive skin, darkened to a richer color by the summer sun. Her thick, shoulder-length black hair was pulled behind her head, the clip inserted vertically the way Israeli women prefer. She'd first come to see him shortly after he'd returned from London. Her initiative surprised him. The last time they'd seen each other was in her apartment on Mount Scopus, the day he was recruited to go to Russia. He'd left early in the morning before she'd wakened—without a word of explanation, without leaving a note.

He'd spoken to her on the phone a few times after that, but that was all.

They had tried to make love the first afternoon she'd appeared at his apartment. He'd lain beside her feeling the soft erection of her nipples, the wetness between her legs; but when she pulled him over her, his body failed him. She attempted to help, using her fingers, her mouth—to no avail. Her tongue could not reach into his mind. They'd tried several times after that, with the same result. She suggested they refrain for a while; if there was no pressure soon everything would return to normal. It struck Steve how much she must care about him.

Dahlia moved across the stone floor, leaving the door open to air out the room. She held a net shopping bag full of tomatoes, cucumbers, cheese, and fresh rolls. Putting it in the corner, she sat on the edge of the bed.

"I just came from Mahane Yehuda," she said. "The rolls are still warm. I'll make some breakfast."

"All right."

She ran her hand along the side of his face. For some reason he cringed. She said nothing. He didn't know if she had felt him recoil at her touch, but he suspected she had.

As he pulled on the clothes thrown over the chair, the shirt heavy with dry sweat, Dahlia moved into the alcove by the door that served as kitchen and eating area. As she sliced the cucumbers and tomatoes she talked to Steve about the summer school classes she was taking on Mount Scopus. He listened and responded with the surface of his brain. In its inner chambers he listened to Susan and heard himself reply. He watched her dressing in the hotel in Moscow. He moved close, touched the softness of her hair. His arms circled her waist, rose to the small of her back. She kissed his ear. . . . He idealized everything about her—forgot that she was an agent, he her assignment.

The image vanished.

"I'm not very hungry," Steve said, sitting at the small table fitted in the corner between the refrigerator and the wall.

"Neither am I." Dahlia smiled and lifted a small slice of cucumber to her mouth.

He moved the food around on his plate. The sounds of her chewing bothered him. He ripped a roll in half, almost attacking it. She sensed his mood but knew she should say nothing. Soothing words would irritate him. She hoped her presence, communicating that he wasn't alone, would help. Slowly she lifted her cup and sipped the lukewarm coffee.

The little noise she made fell like an avalanche of sound against his nerves. He stabbed at the vegetables, held the fork in the air, his muscles tense, his arm quivering. He wanted to throw the fork, to take his plate and send it smashing against the wall, to pick up the table and . . .

He sat there, holding the fork in the air, his whole arm shaking.

"Throw it," Dahlia said.

He saw the lines of tension on her face.

"Throw it."

He hesitated, his shoulder muscles hurting. A second later he lowered his arm. The fork clattered onto the table.

"You should have thrown it," she said.

He looked at her, his gaze distant. "What time's your first class?"

She checked her watch. "In half an hour."

There was silence. Their eyes didn't meet.

"I guess I'd better go," she said finally.

"You don't want to be late."

She took a roll and moved toward the door.

"Wait," he said suddenly. "How about a movie tonight?"

She stopped and turned, her lips lifting into a faint smile.

"How about the Woody Allen film? It's playing at the Eden. We could walk."

"I'd like that," she said.

"Then let's meet here, at eight."

"All right." Her smile widening, she hurried up the stairs into the warm morning. As she headed out the alley toward King George Street she felt a faint sense of hope.

Mark Abrams, the young American turned Israeli who'd first recruited Steve at the Hebrew University, waited for Dahlia in back of the amphitheater atop Mount Scopus. As she approached he peered out over the gorge. The barren hills, broken by deep ravines winding down the rocky slopes to the Dead Sea, blazed in the morning light. The sea itself shone as the sun touched its water.

Looking back at the olive-skinned girl, Mark felt frustrated. He wanted to take her to lunch, to talk to her about something besides Barth, but he knew that was impossible.

He'd gone to see her as soon as the report came in that Barth was in London and psychologically near collapse. Barth's file showed that he and Dahlia had had a relationship for several months. The Colonel made it clear that he wanted Barth kept from cracking. He'd need help, a companion, and Dahlia was the most suitable candidate.

When Mark approached her, she'd been furious at first, refusing to have anything further to do with Barth. He'd walked out on her. He felt nothing, she said—nothing she could reach. Abrams had been forced to tell her more than he intended: Barth was involved in an operation vital to the security of the State of Israel. He had to be kept from falling apart. They would need her for a while, at least several weeks, possibly longer. Whatever the period, it would be deducted from the time she was obligated to spend in the reserves, at full pay.

Dahlia leaned on the railing next to him. "How is he?" Abrams asked.

"I don't know. About the same." A gust of hot wind blew in from the desert, flapping her blouse against her breasts. "Maybe a little worse."

"In what way?"

"He's bottled up, suffocating." Dahlia hesitated. Though she hated telling him personal things about Steve, after a moment she went on. "This morning some pain reached the surface. He wanted to throw a fork across the room. His arm was shaking but he couldn't do it. He stuffed the feeling back inside."

"Is he near exploding?"

"I don't know."

"Take a guess."

"I don't know," she said loudly. "I'm not a psychiatrist!" She'd grown to care for Barth again—to feel compassion for the tortured person he'd become and resentment toward those she blamed for his condition, Abrams among them. "Why can't you leave him alone?"

"Is he still impotent?"

"Damn you," she said under her breath. "Yes."

Abrams imagined the two of them in bed together. "Do you care about him?"

"That's none of your business."

Everything Dahlia felt registered on her face. Abrams read the strong "yes" there. She would never let him near her.

"Everything that has to do with Barth is my business," he said coldly.

She said nothing.

"Do you think you can keep his condition from deteriorating?" Abrams asked, his tone conciliatory now. He had an assignment to perform.

"Yes."

Abrams relaxed somewhat. "Dahlia, I want to emphasize again how important what you're doing is to the security of Israel. If Barth should become incapacitated it would . . ."

"I know," she interrupted. "You've already explained that." She stared at the Dead Sea below, flat like a slab of slate. The strain of the pretense she was forced to play with Barth showed in her eyes. "When is this going to be over?" she asked.

"We don't know. Soon I hope."

"Is there anything else?"

"No, not now. I'll meet you again next week by the Mamilla Pool in Independence Park. Same time."

"All right."

She turned and walked back through the rows of vacant stone seats, hating herself for what she was doing.

*　　*　　*

Steve sat in the small, enclosed courtyard outside his apartment, reading *Stranger in a Strange Land*. He'd read the book before and the frequent lapses where he read paragraphs or pages without recognizing the words didn't disrupt the flow of the plot, which he remembered fairly well. He sat shirtless on a wood chair, the sun's rays reflecting off the stone walls and floor. His upper body was coated with sweat, a thin trickle running down the cleft in his chest. He was anxious to get tan; for some reason he felt stronger when his skin was bronzed. In a little while he'd walk onto King George Street and get something to eat: a steak in pita, a Goldstar beer, and maybe some ice cream for dessert. Then he'd meet Dahlia and see the Woody Allen movie.

Steve heard the squeak of the rusted hinges on the mailbox outside the gate, followed by the sounds of feet moving down the alley toward the next apartment. He got up and found an internal aerogramme inside the mailbox, bearing no sender's address. Since he had no phone people in other parts of the country were forced to communicate with him by mail.

It took him a few seconds to realize who the letter was from. Then, shaking, he let out a cry of joy. Finally something had worked out right. Andrei was in Israel.

He read the letter three times to make sure he hadn't missed anything. Andrei was in the immigrant absorption center in Mevasseret Zion, a short distance from Jerusalem on the road to Tel Aviv. He'd been in Israel only a few days but would be able to leave the center soon because of his knowledge of Hebrew. He'd be in Jerusalem on July 27, looking for a teaching position. He already had an appointment with a physics professor at the Hebrew University and would stop over and see Steve late in the afternoon, after his meeting.

Steve jumped down the four steps leading to his apartment and ran to get his watch. He had no idea what the day's date was. After searching his desk and end table frantically he spotted the leather-banded self-winding Seiko on the floor underneath his bed. He leaned on one knee and grabbed the watch. The time read three-ten. The date, the 27th.

Thirteen-Moscow

Alexandr Mikhailovich Zavorin sat at his desk leafing through a thick *papra* crammed with letterheads bearing the signatures of foreign government officials. Some years before, one of the satellite services, the Czech STB, perceived that many Westerners receiving a Christmas card consider it socially necessary to send one in return. Czech embassies throughout the world soon began to mail ornate Christmas greetings to government officials and other prominent people. The signatures gathered in response later graced the cover letters of bogus documents, forged memos, and fraudulent literature.

Zavorin was going through the Israeli file, searching for anything that might lead him to the Colonel's identity. The man had a name and if he had a name he had a signature. But the KGB General had never seen that signature. Closing the file, Zavorin took a papirosi from his silver cigarette case, lit it, and inhaled in a long drag that caused the paper to crackle as it burned, then snuffed the cigarette out, three-quarters unsmoked. He stared across the room at the portrait of Pavlik Morozov, the child-hero who informed on his father, enraging the peasants of Gerasimovka, who lynched him. Zavorin had been instrumental in having a statue honoring Pavlik erected in Kiev in 1965.

There was a knock on the door and the Major General turned his attention from the picture, muttering the curse *Eb Tvoyu mat* under his breath. There were rumors that Vyacheslav Menzhinsky, then head of the State Political Directorate, had encouraged the peasants to kill the boy, hoping to make Pavlik a martyr. Whether it was true or not, Zavorin was glad the child had been hanged. He deserved as much.

Zavorin's secretary, Yuri Pirozhkov, entered the ornately furnished room.

Zavorin leaned forward on his elbows. "Yes, Yuri Vasilevich."

"I have something," Pirozhkov said. "We discovered an interesting link to Barth that cannot be coincidence. A man registered as Dmitri Karpov requested a suite on the fifth floor of the Metropole, directly across the hall from the room where we keep foreigners under arrest."

"When did he ask for that particular location?"

"Upon arriving in the Soviet Union—two days before the girl was killed."

"But that proves nothing," Zavorin said loudly. "The timing

invalidates your information. We didn't even know we were going to arrest the boy. Not then."

"I know. That's why the information wasn't presented to you earlier. Colonel Grigorenko came to the same conclusion you did."

"Grigorenko."

"Yes, Comrade General." Pirozhkov chose to call Zavorin by his military rank when he was angry. "Colonel Grigorenko considered the two facts coincidence. I agreed with his suggestion that we not trouble you with an inconclusive report. But I just came across an important piece of evidence. I double-checked the records after Grigorenko and discovered that Karpov left Russia on the same flight as Barth!"

"And Grigorenko knew this?" Zavorin asked, tightening his grip around a pencil, then snapping it in half.

"Apparently."

Zavorin took a fresh pencil and, influenced by the fate of Pavlik Morozov, drew a gallows on the pad before him. "Go on," he said between tight lips.

"I checked with some of our people in London. No Dmitri Karpov cleared British Customs. I think we have to assume he switched passports in flight, and entered England under a false name."

"Either that or he used his real passport and Dmitri Karpov is the alias." Zavorin strummed his fingers against the desk. "Were any of my men on the plane with Barth?"

"No, if you remember, we didn't feel it necessary. We knew Barth would go to David and a full report would follow."

Zavorin pounded the table with a flat palm, angry at himself.

He should have sent a man on the plane regardless. "So Karpov is the killer," he said.

"It looks that way."

"Damn it, Yuri." Zavorin struck the table again. "Who is he? And why did he murder the girl?"

"I don't know, sir."

"Then find out. Quickly."

"Yes, Comrade General. I'll get every available man on it." He moved toward the door.

"Wait," Zavorin snapped. "What about Barth?"

Pirozhkov stopped and turned. "He's arrived in Israel."

As his secretary hurried out of the room Zavorin's expression softened. At least something was proceeding as planned.

In London, after taking Grigorenko to the Tate Gallery to meet David, Wulf went directly to the American Embassy. Unfortunately, Phillip Fleske was in Washington for a meeting. When asked if he wanted to speak to someone else Wulf said no, he would wait until Fleske returned.

They met a week later in the Wimpy Bar on Shaftesbury Avenue in the theater district. Wulf ordered a hamburger with grilled onions and Fleske a chocolate bowler: a donut covered with ice cream, chocolate sauce, and nuts. The abandonment of his diet was linked to his brief stay in Washington and his meeting with the Deputy Director of Plans. His superior had talked for a long time about the problems agents like Fleske face when they remain in the field too long, intimating that often they become a burden. In the end the DDP suggested he resign. Aghast, Fleske refused.

What would he do stateside? Push pencils in some cramped office?

Wulf, who affected cockney as a cover, relinquished the dialect as the Pakistani waiter moved away. "Last week I was at Heathrow picking up Russians when Colonel Petr Grigorenko came through."

Fleske looked down at the bowler. The cold had hardened the chocolate sauce. He tapped it lightly with his spoon and the chocolate cracked, revealing the ice cream beneath.

"Go on," he said, lifting a mound of vanilla to his mouth.

"I took him to a call box, then to the Tate Gallery. I waited at the corner like I was looking for a fare. A few minutes later his contact showed up."

"How'd you recognize him?"

"I knew him." Wulf lifted a fork and held it in midair. His voice sounded strained. "It was David."

"Holy shit! Are you sure?"

"Positive." Wulf nervously rearranged the silverware on the table. "What are we going to do? My entire organization's infiltrated. The Russians know everything about us. Worse, they're directing half our activities."

"Don't panic," Fleske said. "The biggest mistake we could make is to let the Russians know we're onto them." He pushed the chocolate bowler aside. "We have the advantage now, let's not lose it. First, have you told Mike?"

"No, I was afraid he might be involved. When we started and needed someone to train us he was the one who found David."

"What story did David give Michael?"

"He told him he was a British intelligence officer during the war, retired now. It checked out." Wulf looked up at the American. "I've known Mike a long time. We met at a demonstration against the British Union of Fascists. Four of Oswald Mosley's thugs had me cornered in an alley in Stepney Green. They would have beaten me into pulp if Mike hadn't come up and taken on two of them. If he's part . . ." Wulf's voice choked.

"I doubt he is," Fleske said. "Seems unlikely the Russians would have both of them. I'll vet it as best I can but I'd say David's our man. In the meantime, until I have something definite, don't say anything to anyone."

Wulf wiped his eyes. "There's something else. The boy, Barth—it was David's idea that we find a young American and send him to Moscow. That means the Russians set up the whole thing. They wanted him there for some reason."

"Christ almighty. I better let the Israelis know immediately." Fleske pushed back his chair. Eliav would probably want to fly to Tel Aviv with the information as soon as possible. "I'll get back to you. Just hold tight."

As Fleske left the Wimpy Bar, Wulf bit into his thin hamburger, hardly realizing he was eating. He'd existed for the last week solely to see Fleske. Now with that accomplished, there was nothing to do, no place to go. Leaving the hamburger half-eaten, he pushed up his collar and walked out into the cold evening. Hours later he was still walking.

Fourteen-Jerusalem

Joseph Eliav landed at Ben Gurion Airport early the afternoon of the 27th. The previous night Phillip Fleske had informed him that the leak inside the English operation was the man known as David. The same David who had first suggested the Israelis send a young American to Moscow. Eliav did not have to be briefed further. The tumblers clicked into place by themselves. The boy's trip was a KGB-guided operation. The following morning Eliav boarded the first flight to Tel Aviv. The Colonel had to be told.

From the airport he took a taxi to Jerusalem, lost himself in a crowd in front of the Café Atara on Ben Yehuda Street, then jumped on the number nine bus and rode to the rocky valley between the Israeli Museum and the Hebrew University, walking distance from the government structures where the Mossad had its headquarters. After clearing a security check inside the end building he mounted the stairs two at a time, proceeded down the corridor, and entered the Colonel's office.

The Colonel was standing at his window, watching a group of children playing in President's Park. He did not acknowledge Eliav's presence. After a long moment the Colonel turned.

"It's nice to see you, Joseph," he said, lifting the box of cigars off the edge of the desk. "Would you care for one?"

"No, thank you."

"If you don't mind, I'll indulge myself." He removed a yellow aluminum tube, slipped out the cigar, and lit it. "You have a smooth flight?"

"Yes."

"No problems at the airport?" The Colonel settled into his large chair. "I heard the baggage carriers were about to go out on strike."

"They were working when I landed," Eliav said.

"Good." The Colonel flicked a quarter inch of ash into the wastebasket. "You can't imagine what a bother it is trying to coordinate operations abroad when I can't get my agents in and out of the country."

Eliav took the chair across from the desk. Tired after traveling for over seven hours, he was in no mood for the Colonel's talking of trivia, regardless of the reason behind it. "We have a problem," he said flatly.

"I should think so. I wasn't expecting you."

"We've found the leak. It's bigger than I thought—David's been doubled. He's a KGB agent."

"Indeed." The Colonel tasted the cigar in his mouth, and let some smoke drift toward Eliav. "That's a bit of a surprise. Runs the whole operation in London, doesn't he?"

"That's not the worst of it. David initiated the Barth trip; he was the one who suggested I find a young American living here. That means the Russians wanted us to send them someone."

"I wouldn't worry," the Colonel said, letting a slight smile show. "David's recruiting Barth shouldn't present all that much of a problem . . . actually, I've been hoping something like that was the case."

Suddenly the phone rang. The Colonel picked it up and listened. Eliav, dumbfounded, sat there staring at the short balding man. After a few moments he heard the head of Israeli Intelligence say, "Excellent." Then he watched him replace the receiver. A long minute later, as if suddenly remembering he wasn't alone, the Colonel returned to Eliav.

"As long as you're here, Joseph, you may as well come along."

Before Eliav could respond, the Colonel was out the door.

Steve sat in the courtyard outside his apartment, *Stranger in a Strange Land* open on the floor by his feet. Even the pretense of reading was impossible; he couldn't concentrate. Andrei was due any moment. Already he'd showered and changed. There didn't seem to be any further way to pass the time so he just sat there excited, staring at the gate leading to the alley. Periodically he looked at his watch. It was four-thirty. He was surprised that Leora, his upstairs neighbor, was not back from work yet. A waitress at the vegetarian Alpin Restaurant on King George

Street, she always returned home at ten after four. He'd never known her to stray from that pattern. Come to think of it, he hadn't seen her husband all day either. Motti didn't work and was usually in and out half a dozen times before lunch. Strange, Steve thought.

He picked up the book and looked at a few sentences before he remembered he was in no mood for reading. Tossing the paperback onto the stone floor, he listened to the sound the wind made rippling the pages. Just as Andrei walked into the courtyard.

Somehow he seemed taller, his face less childlike than it had appeared in the cheerless apartment in Moscow. Without thinking, Steve jumped up and threw his arms around his friend before breaking the embrace self-consciously.

"Andrei, I can't believe it's you. That you're really here."

"Neither can I," Andrei said. "Before I get out of bed in the morning I almost have to pinch myself to make sure I'm not dreaming."

Steve laughed. "Come inside. I want to show you my place. I have a cot. There's lots of room. Can you stay tonight?"

"Sure, I'd love to."

"Fantastic. We'll go out to dinner, I'll show you the Old City. The Wall is beautiful, it's completely lit up. Afterwards, I'll take you to this all-night Arab bakery. People bring their own eggs, tomato, and cheese and the owner bakes it on pita for them. It's unbelievable. There's usually a lot of Hebrew University students there. Then we can walk along the battlements in the Christian quarter. . . ." Suddenly Steve remembered he had a date with Dahlia. He hesitated for a moment, then decided to leave a note on the door explaining why he wasn't home. It would be all right, she'd understand.

Inside, he went to the refrigerator, pulled out two bottles of beer, and handed one to Andrei. They sat at the narrow table.

Steve took a large gulp of the cold beer. "Tell me about everybody," he said. "What about Fayim?"

"Fayim was denied permission to emigrate," Andrei said.

Steve's face dropped. "Why? What reason did they give?"

"The clerk at the Offices of Visas and Internal Registration said that he had access to state secrets and would not be allowed to take them to the West. We demanded to know what state secrets, Fayim had never worked with any sensitive information. She told us the secrets he handled dealt with highly classified material and could not be discussed. He lodged a protest with the Central Committee of the Communist Party, demanding to know what information he possessed. The following day Fayim was brought in for questioning and told he had a week to find a job. Every place he applied refused to hire him. At the end of the week he was arrested and charged with parasitism. His trial begins next month. He expects to receive a three-year sentence."

Steve mumbled a curse. "Why do they do this? I don't understand. Why did they let you go and arrest him?"

"It's their way. The random harassment of individuals frightens tens of thousands of people on the verge of applying for visas. If they think there's a chance they might go to jail they remain inactive, toeing the Communist line."

Some beer went down the wrong passage and Steve coughed, hard. Then there was silence. Andrei sipped his beer noiselessly. Steve's thoughts slipped back to his own KGB interrogation, to the humiliation that flooded him when Nikolai Prestin confiscated Zev's letter, to the guilt he felt for relinquishing it without a struggle.

"I still feel terrible about Zev's letter," Steve said.

The Russian looked up.

"I hope he didn't get into trouble because of it."

"Zev's dead," Andrei said.

Steve's lips whitened, sweat beaded near his hairline. "No."

"He was called up for military reserve duty and stationed in Arkhara near the Chinese border. A stray bullet struck him in the head during training maneuvers. He died instantly."

"They killed him because of what was in the letter!" Steve cried out.

"No," Andrei said. "It was probably an accident."

"You're lying. The secret police shot him, you know it. You're just trying to make me feel better. I caused his death. It's my fault!" Steve shrieked. "*I killed him.*"

"No, you don't understand," Andrei said quietly, his tone reassuring. "The letter was in Russian, right? Well, I read it and there was nothing there. Nothing. Zev wrote to his brother. He talked about family matters, how his kids were doing in school, how he felt about their separation, how he hoped they would be together soon. He wouldn't have written anything that might jeopardize your safety. Zev wasn't like that and furthermore after reading the letter the Russians let you go. If there was anything there, believe me, they would have held you. I'm sure of that. If the secret police did kill Zev it had nothing to do with the letter."

Steve's breathing slowed somewhat. Andrei made sense. "I guess you're right," he said.

"There's no other possible explanation."

Steve nodded, taking a mouthful of beer. Though he allowed himself to believe Andrei's words, somehow he still felt he was responsible for the bullet that killed Zev.

He finished his beer and tossed the empty bottle three feet into the basket. He'd have another with dinner. "Are you hungry?" he asked, anxious to escape his feelings.

"A little."

"Then why don't we get something to eat." He stood, stretching. "I'd better get you a sweater. Jerusalem's pretty high in the mountains. It gets cold at night, even in summer."

Steve moved across the room toward the small dresser set under the series of Shohar posters, rejects which he'd picked up free from their kibbutz factory near the Mediterranean. His favorite was a blue and gray sketch of Jonah caught inside the body of a whale. He paused to look at it for a moment. Unlike Jonah, the body he felt trapped in was his own.

He pulled open a drawer, searched for a sweater, then stopped. He turned toward Andrei. "Wait a minute, your book. How could I forget?" He reached for the bottom of the drawer, felt something solid, and pulled out the Bible. A smile brightened Andrei's face. "I'm sorry," Steve said anxiously. "The binding's ripped. The KGB interrogator, he came to the hotel and searched my belongings. He found the Bible, rifled the pages, and threw it on the floor. There was nothing I could do."

"Please, Steve, I understand. It's a miracle that you were able to get it out of Russia at all." Andrei took the Bible and tucked it under his arm. "Did the interrogator ask if the book had been given to you by anyone in Moscow?"

"No. He seemed to assume it was mine."

Andrei nodded, pleased. "The secret police often ignore the obvious. The dissidents joke that it's easier to smuggle an elephant out of Russia than a roll of microfilm. The KGB can be very haphazard about certain things."

"And very thorough about others," a voice said from behind them.

Andrei turned.

The short, pudgy frame of the man who spoke was silhouetted in the doorway. The Colonel moved into the room followed by Eliav and a tall, powerfully built security officer. They had temporarily removed Barth's neighbors in order to monitor the conversation through speakers wired into the upstairs rooms.

"Who are you? What are you doing in my apartment?" Steve asked angrily.

Not bothering to answer, the Colonel stopped inches from Andrei. "What do we have here?" He removed the book from the boy's grip. "A Hebrew Bible, Russian no doubt." He flipped open the cover, saw the title page was missing and looked up at Andrei. "I have a collection of Russian Bibles, but this one looks rather special. You don't mind if I keep it, do you?"

"Who do you think you are?" Steve protested loudly. "You can't take that. It's his. I brought it out of Russia so the KGB wouldn't confiscate it. It's a family heirloom. The book means a lot to him."

"I bet it does," the Colonel said. "But I doubt it's been in his family very long."

Steve reached for the Bible, grabbing a handful of air as the Colonel sidestepped him.

"You'd better give it back to me," Steve threatened, "or I'll get the police."

"Don't trouble yourself." The Colonel sounded amused. "We are the police."

The indignant expression fell from Steve's face. "What?"

"Steve, I'm afraid you've been duped by the Russians. Your

friend is not who he appears to be." The Colonel watched Andrei. "He cares nothing for this country or for you. Andrei is a KGB agent."

"What are you talking about?" Andrei said. He stared at the Colonel. "You're crazy."

"Don't bother to deny it. We know you're not Jewish."

"You're a goddamn liar," Andrei shouted. "I am Jewish. I'm as Jewish as you are."

"Please don't tell me you've been circumcised—everybody's circumcised these days."

"I was Bar Mitzvahed."

"Sure you were."

"Give me the Bible," Andrei demanded. "Let me read to you. That'll prove I was one of the Hebrew teachers in Moscow."

"Oh, I don't doubt that you were. In fact, I understand you are one of the more proficient in Hebrew. Section S of the First Chief Directorate is the language instruction department of the KGB. On the second floor of the Center, isn't it?"

"Why ask me? How would I know? The only time I was in KGB headquarters is when they interrogated me about the Viktor Polsky trial."

"That's strange," the Colonel said. "I had you followed after you met Steve in the Metropole. You went to a phone box on Ulitza Trubnaya, called the American Embassy to protect your cover, then went to two Dzerzhinsky Square, entered the building, and reported to your KGB superiors to discuss what Steve had told you."

Sweat broke out on Andrei's brow and the taste of bile choked his throat. It was true. After speaking to the American ambassador he had gone directly to see Alexandr Mikhailovich Zavorin.

"In Vienna, Israeli security thoroughly searches every article a Russian immigrant brings from the Soviet Union," the Colonel said, turning to Steve. "Knowing that, our friend Andrei needed to protect himself. He didn't want the Bible looked at too closely, so he made you his courier." The Mossad chief tapped the book with a stubby finger. "Apparently there's something in here he didn't want us to find."

The Colonel held the Bible up to the light, testing for double pages, for invisible ink, for something secured in the binding—all to no avail. He paused a moment and looked at the book with his mind. Why had the KGB used such a bulky volume? What was special about a Bible? How did it differ from other Hebrew books?

Suddenly he knew. The answer, flashing into his brain, seemed so obvious. Modern Hebrew texts and newspapers were currently printed without vowels, the dots below the letters. The Colonel's face was expressionless as he turned to Eliav. "Microdots. Below the Hebrew letters, on top of the vowels, there have to be microdots." He closed the book gently. "That's how the KGB's been communicating with their agents. They've been sending microdot-filled Hebrew texts in and out of the Soviet Union. It's probably been going on for years, right under our noses."

"I bet the books Steve took to Moscow were tampered with in London," Eliav said. "If David put a microdot message in them, the Russians would have known that Susan was a CIA agent."

Shaken, his knees trembling, Steve stared at the man who spoke from the darkness behind the Colonel. He looked familiar. Steve thought he'd seen the face somewhere in Moscow but that was impossible. As he looked hard the face blurred. He shut his eyes; nothing cleared in his head. Andrei, Susan, microdots, the

Israeli secret service, Zev, Dahlia, this new face. Images raced in his brain, coming faster and faster, one on top of the other.

Andrei, too, looked at the man hidden behind the Colonel. He took a few steps closer, stared at his features for a disbelieving moment—then everything tumbled together. Grigorenko had shown him Eliav's picture along with the Colonel's the day he left Moscow. In the dim light he hadn't recognized the man earlier. Now he understood. The last piece of the mosaic slipped into place, bringing the entire picture into focus.

Andrei had asked himself how the Colonel could have broken his cover. He'd been a Hebrew teacher, an unsuspected member of the Jewish dissidents, for over three years. Nobody had ever challenged his allegiance to the Zionist movement. He'd mailed his weekly reports to a special address, personally. He'd remained unseen, burying himself deeper in the flesh of the Jewish cause, waiting, preparing for eventual immigration to Israel, for the unfolding of Operation Cloverleaf. The Colonel had spoiled his moment of triumph, squashed the success that would have made the last three years bearable. Now, knowing how, he stared at the head of Israeli Intelligence and spoke quietly. "Nobody suspected it, but you ordered Susan killed, didn't you? That's how you identified me."

The Colonel showed a small smile.

Steve screamed. The room spun inside his head. He lost his breath. Andrei ignored him. "You had Susan killed so the KGB would arrest Steve. You knew foreigners are interrogated in a special room on the fifth floor of the Metropole and you knew the KGB sends agents, masquerading as friends, to talk to them in the lavatory across from that room. With the American government certain to put pressure on Moscow protesting the mysterious killing of a young girl and Steve, of course, unable to give his interrogator any information, you felt confident the KGB would send an agent to find out what he knew about the girl's death. You surmised correctly that we would send the only person Steve would trust—the agent infiltrated among the Hebrew teachers he had met earlier—me." Andrei moved closer to the Colonel. "One thing I don't understand. What made you suspect one of the Hebrew teachers was working for the KGB?"

"Earlier in the year when the Hebrew classes were raided and the books confiscated so systematically, we knew there had to be an informer," the Colonel said. "When we learned that the KGB was about to activate their sleepers in the Israeli army we assumed the agent deeply hidden among the Hebrew teachers would be the least suspect and thus the most likely to be sent to conduct the operation."

"Very clever, all of it. You recognized where the agent was planted, so you had Susan killed knowing that the operative you needed to identify would be sent to the hotel to interrogate Steve under the guise of offering him help. All the while the real killer was down the hall, with his door open just wide enough to get a good look at me as I left the lavatory." Andrei turned to Eliav, studying his features. "Isn't that the way it was—Dmitri Karpov? You followed me to KGB headquarters."

"I'm afraid so," Eliav said softly. "But I really didn't need to see you walk into the Center. Your being allowed in the bathroom was proof enough."

Steve listened to their voices from the distance. What were they talking about? A girl was dead. Someone named Susan. He couldn't remember. He thought he knew a Susan, but that seemed a long time ago, in another place. She couldn't be dead.

He tried to recall. Maybe she never existed. He didn't know, didn't remember.

Steve listened hard, trying to understand the voices around him; but each successive second they seemed more detached, more distant. There was a throbbing in his head and he felt warm and damp. His clothes stuck to his skin. He opened his mouth and tried to speak but no words came out. The pulsing in his head intensified, pounding the inside of his skull. A young Russian-looking man near him was talking. Steve lifted his arm; it felt heavy, difficult to move. He reached toward the voice but never made it. The room blurred. The sounds were gone. He fell to the floor unconscious.

Fifteen-Jerusalem

Morning sunlight, pouring through the open window, fell across the bed, waking Steve. He lifted himself on his elbows and studied his new surroundings: the white enamel walls, empty dresser, and end table with flowerless vase. He didn't know where he was, didn't remember leaving his apartment. In fact he didn't seem to remember much of anything about the previous day. He'd had breakfast with Dahlia, they'd talked about going to see a movie, but everything after that was blank. He strained, trying to pull the past into the present—without success. He didn't think they had gone to the movie, but he wasn't sure.

Steve pushed the starched sheets aside and lowered himself off the bed. Groggy, he had to grab on to the metal frame for support. He stood there awhile, his bare feet cold against the floor. Slowly, he made his way to the window; a flood of sunlight bathed him in its warmth. He saw that the building was at the bottom of a vast valley. On either side rose terraced vineyards and olive groves. To the right, in a small grove on the summit of Mount Orah, was a domed chapel, barely visible; on the left, the Swedish-built children's home. Below, nestled on a hillside of tall cypresses and olive groves, Steve recognized the village of Ein Karem. He was in Hadassah Hospital.

He sat on the edge of the bed, wondering how he'd got to the hospital and why. For a moment he thought he'd had an accident, but he felt all right, nothing seemed wrong with him. He considered finding someone to ask but, deciding against such a move, stretched out on the bed. A strange calm had enveloped him; he had no desire to disrupt it.

Sometime later the sound of the door opening jarred him out of a light sleep. He opened his eyes expecting to see a nurse or doctor, only to be greeted by Dahlia, carrying a breakfast tray. She placed it on the bedside table and sat on the edge of the mattress, taking his hand. Her fingers felt dry and cool.

"How are you?" she asked.

He watched her face. "Okay, I guess. It doesn't seem anything's wrong with me." He raised himself on his elbows. "Dahlia, why am I here?"

Fighting tears, she looked away, focusing her attention on the tray. "You'd better eat something. You didn't have dinner last night."

He did feel a little weak. Maybe food would help. "All right," he said.

There was a morning *Jerusalem Post* by the plastic cup of coffee. Steve put the newspaper on the table and balanced the tray on his lap. The scrambled eggs were watery. They tasted processed. He ate a few mouthfuls, then turned to Dahlia.

"How did I get here?"

"I brought you in a taxi. When I got to your apartment last night the door was open and you were lying on the floor." She bit her lower lip. "You were hardly breathing. At first I thought you were dead. I thought you might have taken something and . . ." Her face became ashen. "Steve, what happened?"

"I don't know." He put the tray back on the end table. The scene she described felt unfamiliar. "The last thing I remember is sitting in the courtyard reading. I think I was waiting for someone . . . you, I guess. Everything afterwards is blank."

"You don't remember what happened?"

"No."

Dahlia fingered her long hair, pulling it over her shoulder. "Maybe a friend came over, someone you weren't expecting?"

Steve thought hard. "I don't know." Suddenly he slammed his fist down. "I can't remember. I can't remember anything!"

Dahlia held him in her arms. "It's all right. Try and relax. You'll be fine. Whatever it is, I'm sure it'll come back to you, eventually."

For some unknown reason, her touch triggered the tension locked inside him. He pushed her away. "Dahlia, will you get a doctor? I want to find out what's the matter with me."

"Okay." She moved toward the door, opened it, and turned.

"I'll wait and come back when he's done . . . that is, if you want me to."

"Fine," he said.

As the door closed behind her, Steve lay back against the pillow. Why couldn't he remember anything? Restlessly he grabbed the *Jerusalem Post* and opened it to the front page. He'd removed his mind from the dilemma until the doctor came.

High in the center of the page was a photograph of a young man about Steve's age. Though Steve didn't think he knew him, his face looked vaguely familiar. The headline over the picture read:

RUSSIAN IMMIGRANT COMMITS SUICIDE

MEVASSERET ZION—Andrei Bukharov, 23, a recent immigrant from Moscow, was found dead in his room at the absorption center in Mevasseret Zion late last night, an apparent suicide. Bukharov, a long-time dissident active in Jewish circles in the Soviet Union, had become despondent recently, friends in the absorption center testified. He was found at approximately 1:00 A.M. by Yuli Rivlin, an immigrant from Odessa. Rivlin, who lives next door to Bukharov, heard the water overflowing in his neighbor's sink. When there was no answer at the front door Rivlin broke the lock and entered the room. He found the deceased on the bathroom floor, his wrists slit. An ambulance was summoned but Bukharov was pronounced dead on arrival at Hadassah Hospital in Jerusalem.

Outwardly the young Russian appeared to be adjusting well to his new life in Israel. However observers noted that in private moments he was increasingly depressed over the recent death of Zev Zaretsky and the lengthy imprisonment of Fayim Orlov, both long-time friends. Neighbors mentioned that the young man seemed tortured by guilt for having reached Israel while his friends suffered such disastrous fates. Authorities speculated that these feelings may have caused him to take his life.

Andrei Bukharov, a former Candidate in physics at the Lebedev Institute of the Russian Academy of Sciences, arrived in Israel only six days prior to his death. He is survived by an uncle, Boris Bukharov, living in Rostov-on-Don . . .

Steve screamed. Not understanding what the story meant to him, why he was in the hospital, what was happening, anything—he screamed. He ripped at the paper, shredding the newsprint, shrieking. The noise echoed down the corridor. Nobody heard. Nobody came. His throat raw, he continued to scream. Pulse racing, his head grew light. Though his mouth remained open, he no longer heard his own voice.

The door burst open. Dahlia and a doctor ran into the room. She remained near the entrance, her body pressed against the wall. A thin trickle of tears ran along her nose and down the side of her mouth. The doctor grabbed Steve's upper arm. Slipping a needle under the boy's skin he injected 75 milligrams of Thorazine.

Steve stared at the doctor, at Dahlia. Their movements seemed so slow. He closed his eyes. The ceiling spun. The floor seemed to pitch beneath him, and suddenly he was cold, very cold. Susan's face flashed in his mind and then it was gone. As he fell against the pillow, there was only blackness.

Joseph Eliav walked through the pale yellow corridors of Mossad headquarters, not caring who noticed him. The Colonel, attempting to involve as few people as possible, had asked him to kill Andrei Bukharov. In answer, Eliav had walked away. He supposed that the old man had completed the task personally.

Eliav entered the Colonel's sparsely furnished office without knocking. The head of the Israeli Intelligence, seated at his desk, continued to write, without looking up. "Shamir in Operational Planning gave me a message for you," Eliav said, not waiting for the Colonel's attention. "Somebody broke in and searched Andrei's room in the absorption center this morning, right after the suicide story broke in *Yediot Achronot* and the *Jerusalem Post*."

The Colonel leaned back in the chair. "Anything missing?"

"Some of his clothes . . . and, as you suspected, the Bible."

"Excellent," the Colonel said. "With any luck it will arrive in Moscow tomorrow."

"With the microdots in place?"

The Colonel smiled. "No sense tipping our hand to the Russians. They'll know we had something to do with Bukharov's death. What remains is to convince them we arrested the boy and he killed himself, *before* being forced to reveal what he knew."

"That means you can't pick up the sleeper agents."

"Unfortunately, their disappearance would alert Moscow that we'd discovered the microdots. We'll have to be content with watching them. For the time being, anyway."

"Will the Russians buy it? Even though they retrieved the book apparently untouched, won't they suspect we tampered with the microdots?"

"They might," the Colonel said, "but I think I've found a way to convince them we didn't."

Eliav took the chair opposite the desk and sat down. Successfully persuading the KGB that their communications network was still intact would be a major intelligence coup. If messages could be intercepted, decoded, and replaced without the Soviets' knowledge, an advantage in the invisible war of espionage would tilt toward the West. "The microdots, I assume, contained the list of sleeper agents, their locations, and the individual code phrases with times and places for activating them."

The Colonel nodded. "Rather a complete accounting, the lab boys tell me."

Eliav looked away, watching wisps of cirrus clouds move past the window. "What about Barth?" he asked.

The Colonel reached for a cigar tube and slowly unscrewed the top. "Unfortunately he saw the story about Andrei in the morning papers. He became hysterical. They had to sedate him. He should sleep most of the afternoon."

"I see . . . and his memory?"

"Gone, Dahlia reports. Apparently he forgot everything he heard. He doesn't even remember who Susan was." The Colonel paused to light his cigar. "This may turn out for the best," he said between puffs. "His loss of memory, that is."

"Best for us, but what about him?" Eliav's anger sharpened his tone. "Comrade General Zavorin doesn't know about his loss of memory and wouldn't believe it if we leaked the truth. The boy learned too much."

The Colonel rested his cigar in an ashtray. "I know."

"Zavorin will be after him. He'll want to know what happened to Andrei, and Steve's his only lead."

"The possibility occurred to me," the Colonel said. "I'd like to get Barth out of the country immediately. Israel will be the first place the KGB will look for him."

"I have some friends at Claybury Hospital outside London. It's a mental sanitarium off the main roads. He'll be safe there."

"As long as we don't let David know where he is," the Colonel reminded him.

Eliav, aware of the obvious, said nothing.

The Colonel, sensing Eliav's mood, leaned forward in his chair. "Joseph, I don't like this business anymore than you. But I do what I do for a reason: it's the only way to achieve results. We have no choice. If we don't achieve results we die."

Eliav looked at his mentor for a hard moment. "Maybe sometimes it's better to die."

"You think so," the Colonel said, snuffing out his cigar.

"I'm beginning to."

"What about Barth? Should we just let the KGB have him? Does he deserve to die?"

A mantle of sadness settled over Eliav. The Colonel had brought him into such a cheerless world, one with so few options, so little chance of dignity. "No," he said. "Not after what he's been through."

"Then let's hope his memory doesn't return."

Silence filled the room. There was no response.

"I'll schedule a flight," the Colonel said. "To Gatwick Airport. Don't want to take a chance on Heathrow, the Russians may be watching it. You'll accompany him."

"No," Eliav said flatly. "I think not. I'll arrange everything from here, but I'm not going to London or anywhere else for that matter. I'm afraid I'm through."

"I see," the Colonel said. If the Mossad chief was taken by surprise he didn't show it. "You know I have nobody else as good at this sort of thing."

"Then find someone, or train a new recruit. Somebody younger. There are plenty of people out there with nothing, willing to give their all for the service. You'll find a suitable candidate. You always do."

"I suppose I will," the Colonel said, relighting his cigar. "You'll at least go to London and see Fleske. Since Barth's an American he'll have to be briefed."

Eliav smiled. The Colonel was trying to lure him back into the field, hoping once there he'd taste familiar surroundings, smell the closeness of the other side, and want to stay. The approach had worked before and Eliav knew he was as susceptible to it as anyone.

"No," he said. "You'll have to find another agent."

"There's nobody else I can trust with this."

"Then go yourself," Eliav said.

He rose slowly, knowing he would never see the Colonel again. He would have liked to say something, to end their association with a touch of warmth, with some act of meaning. But there was nothing to say. Silently he left the room, listening to the sound of his footsteps in the empty corridors.

September 1

Sixteen-Vienna, London

The Colonel left Phillip Fleske in the Stadtpark, crossed Weiskirchnerstrasse, and entered the lobby of Vienna's Hilton Hotel. At the kiosk near the registration desk he bought a roll of American antacids. He chewed two of the chalky tablets. They seemed to have no effect whatsoever.

In one of the small telephone booths lining the wall on the lower level of the hotel he reached the overseas operator and placed a call to a previously unused number in London. The phone was answered immediately.

"Hello."

"Fleske's on his way to England," the Colonel said quietly.

"When?"

"The ten-forty flight, British Airways. You'll have to check the exact arrival time." The Colonel paused. "Zavorin will be following him."

The voice at the other end waited a second before responding. "I see. Is there anything else?"

"No."

The Colonel hung up and checked his watch. He had three hours before his return flight to Tel Aviv.

As the British Airways Trident jet crossed the cliffs of Dover descending toward London, Phillip Fleske leaned back in his seat. In the warm womb of the plane he thought about his boys, ages nineteen and twenty-three—Barth's age—safe in Virginia far from the influence of the life he led. After the divorce he'd remained on good terms with his wife; they didn't care enough about each other to make things difficult. The boys thought their father worked for the State Department.

The plane began its landing approach across the small fields west of Stanwell. Fleske fastened his seatbelt and reviewed in his mind his meeting with the Colonel. He was surprised the Mossad chief had left Israel and flown to Austria. With Eliav's abrupt departure from the service the Colonel must have wanted to oversee the end of this Barth business personally. The bastard doesn't trust anybody, Fleske thought, somewhat amused. That must make his life a bit lonely.

Like the Colonel, Fleske had been worried about the gradual return of Barth's memory. The boy had begun asking to see Susan. They could stall him only so long. Soon they would have to tell him she was dead and that might snap everything into place. He knew something would have to be done but it wasn't until the Colonel pronounced similar sentiments that his conscious mind faced the realization that they would have to kill Barth. The boy had learned too much—he suspected Andrei hadn't committed suicide and worse, he knew the Israelis had uncovered the Russian microdot transmission system, a network all Western intelligence services wanted the KGB to think was unbroken. If the Soviets got hold of Steve, in his present condition he'd tell them everything.

In sum, Barth presented too great a threat. He had to be eliminated. There was no other alternative.

Fleske was jolted from his thoughts as the wheels struck the smooth tarmac. Flaps down, the plane surged forward in the air, bounced twice, then slowed as the pilot pulled back on the throttle.

Fleske left the aircraft and entered the terminal, unaware that the quiet passenger sitting a dozen rows to his rear had followed him from Vienna. Alexandr Mikhailovich Zavorin, his hair clipped short, his face disguised by a three-day-old salt-and-pepper beard, dropped back in the crowd. He did not need to keep Fleske in sight. One of Zavorin's Viennese agents, posing as a maid, had entered the American's room in the Bristol Hotel and coated his shoes with a chemical that registered on a receiver within a twenty-mile radius. David would be waiting in a Rover equipped with a special monitoring device. They would drop back in traffic and if the East German Intelligence report was correct, Fleske would lead him directly to Steve Barth. Zavorin merely had to stay close enough to prevent Fleske from killing the boy.

When the Abteilung first informed the KGB that the Colonel and Fleske were planning to kill Barth the news had bothered

Zavorin. He wanted to know why. Why was the boy so important? What had he learned in Jerusalem? Zavorin concluded that Barth had discovered something crucial. The Israelis must feel he was not reliable, that if the other side questioned him he'd spill everything he knew. What Zavorin had to do, then, was clear. As soon as the boy's location was positively identified, he would eliminate Fleske, drug the boy, and take him to the safe-house David had prepared. Once he talked, Zavorin would let Barth go. There would be no point in killing him.

After clearing the airport formalities, Phillip Fleske climbed in the first cab queued in the rank outside the terminal, keeping his small suitcase in the back seat with him. He gave the driver instructions, coughing as he spoke the name of a main intersection in Whitechapel near the anonymous side street where his car was parked. The driver nodded and thrust the taxi into gear.

As the big cab barreled along the M4 Motorway, Fleske's thoughts drifted back to the days after Andrei's death and the quick, silent transfer of Barth to Claybury Hospital. In Eliav's absence Mark Abrams, the agent who had accompanied Steve to London, briefed him about what had happened in Jerusalem. He said that the Colonel had assumed that the KGB would attempt to recover Andrei's Bible, so he had replaced the microdots over the points where he'd found them. Though Andrei's room was broken into, the Bible stolen and forwarded to Moscow, both the Mossad and the CIA were concerned that the KGB would suspect that the Colonel had in fact uncovered their communications system. The Russians had to be convinced that the Mossad knew nothing. That's where Fleske came in. Abrams had asked him to go to Michael Marks with a phony story, reporting that he'd just had word from Jerusalem about Andrei Bukharov's purported suicide.

Bukharov had indeed committed suicide, Fleske was to explain, but not for the reasons printed in the Israeli papers. Somehow the Colonel, discovering he was a KGB agent, had arrested him. While waiting in his cell to be interrogated, Bukharov killed himself with a capsule of cyanide he had hidden up his anal tract. Apparently he knew something important and was afraid the Israelis would force him to talk. All friendly services were being alerted—the Colonel suspected Bukharov was part of a major KGB operation, whose particulars were still unknown.

Fleske looked out the taxi window, watching the red tile roofs of the houses below the motorway. The Colonel counted on Marks to relay everything he'd been told to David, who in due course would forward the information to Moscow. David's report, coupled with the apparently untouched Bible, would convince the KGB that their system of transmitting microdot messages through Hebrew books had not been broken. David's duplicity would be turned into a valuable asset.

Fleske told the cab driver to drop him in front of the Blind Beggar Public House on Mile End Road; he'd walk the few short blocks to Collingwood Street where his Opel Rekord was parked. No sense letting the cabbie see his car. Minutes later he pulled into the traffic flowing east on Mile End Road. Checking other cars and drivers, as he had repeatedly since leaving the airport, he saw nothing suspicious. He assumed no one was following him. After slowing to circle Stratford Church, a Gothic anachronism on an island in the center of the street, he raced past Maryland Point Station, and entered Leytonstone Road. The traffic was light; he'd reach Claybury Hospital in another fifteen, twenty minutes.

One thing about this whole business still puzzled him— Susan's death. She was sent into the Soviet Union to lend the boy support, to provoke his pride into resisting if interrogated. She wasn't supposed to do anything and she wasn't supposed to get killed. The Colonel said he suspected the Russians killed her for some reason of their own. But Fleske wondered. Granted that David tampered with the books the two of them brought Zaretsky, placing a microdot message in the Hebrew texts to identify Susan as a CIA agent, and that, as a matter of course, Andrei had lifted the message and passed it to Zavorin or Grigorenko—why would they kill her? For what reason? Every time Fleske traveled this line of thinking he reached the same conclusion: they wouldn't. He remembered Eliav casually mentioning that it might be a good idea to send a girl into the Soviet Union to accompany Barth, someone with experience. At the time Fleske had thought the suggestion sound, but now he wondered. The Colonel could have been setting him up, requesting the CIA provide him with a lamb sheared for slaughter. With growing anger, he realized the Israelis must have killed the girl. Now, he had to prove it.

Back out of sight, David drove in silence as Zavorin watched the monitor attached to the space where the cigarette lighter should have been. It had a small black screen with concentric red lines marking off the miles and a green blip indicating the position of the target.

"Any idea where he's going?" Zavorin asked.

"He should reach Wanstead Hospital on Hermon Hill Road in a few minutes. That could be it."

Zavorin peered through the windshield, making sure they did not come into visual contact with Fleske's green Rekord. Now that they were so close, he wanted to be careful not to alert the American and blow everything.

"If you hadn't contacted me, Grigorenko might have succeeded," Zavorin said, diverting his eyes momentarily to the floor
where the 9mm Baretta pistol David had provided him lay. It had
a silencer screwed on the end of its barrel. "With your support he
could have convinced the Collegium that I had the girl murdered,
counting on her death to infuriate the Americans and weaken
detente. My position on that subject is, unfortunately, too well
known. Brezhnev would have sent me packing. Despite his hard
line he still wants an arms limitation pact."

"Where is Grigorenko now?" David asked, navigating the
roundabout across from the Green Man Pub.

"In Lefortovo Prison. At first he was rather uncooperative.
He kept claiming that he didn't know who Dmitri Karpov was, that
he didn't hire him to kill the girl. He insisted that once he'd
discovered that an unidentified agent, this Karpov, murdered the
girl, he'd decided to exploit the opportunity and make it look like
the killer was in my employ. Grigorenko is stronger than I
thought. He stuck to that story for over three weeks, under, shall I
say, not the most pleasant physical conditions. In the end he
signed a full confession. He'll go on trial as soon as he . . . heals."

David smiled, certain now that he'd made the right decision
in exposing Grigorenko. The Major General was already in a
position to provide certain services. Grigorenko's status had been
tenuous, and even if Zavorin had been demoted, there was no
guarantee that Grigorenko would have been upgraded to a rank
equaling Zavorin's. Grigorenko simply did not have *blat*, influence in the right places. David, Russian-born, an officer in Special
Services II, the Counterintelligence Department of the First
Directorate of the KGB, had had enough—on the tails of thirty
years in the West he was anxious to return home. Once Zavorin

had questioned Barth about Andrei and the Bible, David planned to request payment for his help—reassignment to Dzerzhinsky Square.

They passed a red brick Victorian building and a sign reading WANSTEAD HOSPITAL. "Where is he now?" Zavorin asked.

"He's turned into Chigwell Road," David said. "That creates two possibilities. Either he'll hook up with the motorway and head north, or he'll turn and proceed through Woodford Bridge."

"What's there?"

"Claybury Hospital. It's a mental sanitarium."

Zavorin reached for the Baretta and tucked the pistol in his coat pocket. It was almost time.

Phillip Fleske approached the twin gatehouses flanking the entrance to the thousand-acre hospital grounds. Once the servant quarters of Claybury Manor, they had been linked by tall wrought-iron gates, which were turned into ammunition during the war and never replaced. There was no guard to question his presence so Fleske continued onto the grounds, driving up the long, tree-lined road toward the inmates' building. To his right were neatly manicured rows of yellow, pink, and red roses—to his left, a stretch of grass, edged by weeping willows. Behind the drooping trees were stately horse chestnuts, majestic in size. Fleske parked his car behind the three-story building housing the voluntary patients. Prisoners committed by the authorities as well as those considered dangerously insane were kept in specially secured buildings near the copse in the back of the manor.

The American stared at the large red-brick turreted structure that had been Steve's home since he'd arrived in London. Its tall windows needed painting, the white frames had turned gray. He crossed the lawn where groups of the voluntary patients were seated, talking, and headed up the stone steps into the building. Seconds later Alexandr Mikhailovich Zavorin drove onto the grounds, alone. He'd left David at a bus stop on Manor Road. The fat man's physical features were too recognizable for him to risk entering the hospital.

Fleske climbed the stairs to the third floor, short of breath and coughing lightly. He proceeded down the high-ceilinged, sterile white corridor to the end room. The hallway was empty save for a single man seated in front of the door he sought, reading a paperback Agatha Christie. Fleske stopped in front of him.

"Is the boy inside, Harry?"

"Sleeping," the man said, without looking up from the page.

Fleske nodded. He eased the door open a crack. Fully clothed, Steve lay asleep on the bed, in front of a bay window. Fleske shut the door and turned back to Harry Dunn, one of the three bodyguards who rotated watch over Barth.

"You can go now. We won't be needing your services anymore."

Dunn closed the book. "Suits me fine. This place makes my skin crawl. A guy could go looney just hanging around here."

As Dunn moved down the hall Fleske entered the small nurse's station across the corridor. With a special key, he opened a bottom drawer, reached under a stack of towels, pulled out a small box, and flipped it open, extracting a syringe and a vial of potassium. Pushing the needle through the rubber-topped vial he filled the syringe with a hundred milliequivalents of the colorless alkali. The kit had been stored there when Steve had arrived at the hospital—in the event it was needed, quickly.

Outside, Alexandr Zavorin spotted the green Rekord David

had identified as belonging to Fleske. He pulled his vehicle alongside and hurried across the grass to where a group of seemingly sane patients were playing cards. It would take him too long to search the huge three-story building; the boy might be dead before he located him. Zavorin stopped just short of the group of men and bent on one knee. He knew people often feel intimidated when strangers stand over them.

"Any of you guys know my nephew?" he asked in a precisely practiced accent. "Steven Barth. He's in his early twenties, blondish, with a red beard. They gave me his room number but I can't seem to find the slip of paper I wrote it on."

There was a long silence.

Zavorin pulled a pack of cigarettes from his shirt pocket and tossed it on the grass in the middle of the circle.

"He must be the kid up on the third floor," a thin balding man said, reaching for the cigarettes. "At the end of the corridor on the right, the American."

"Thanks," Zavorin nodded. "I'm sure that's him."

He walked toward the building at a normal pace, but on entering the empty first-floor hallway he bolted up the stairs, three at a time, halting abruptly as he met Harry Dunn on the second-floor landing. He'd spotted the shoulder pistol outlined under the man's coat.

"Good day," Zavorin said, seizing the initiative, as if at home in the hospital.

"What's so good about it?" Dunn passed him and continued down the stairs.

Zavorin climbed the steps slowly until Dunn was out of sight, then began to run again.

Phillip Fleske left the nurse's station, moved across the hall, and entered Steve's room. As he closed the door behind him, the boy stirred. Fleske remained rigid. It would be so easy if the boy stayed asleep. Another sound might wake him.

Steve tossed inside a dream. He was in KGB headquarters in Moscow, the interrogator saying something about Susan. He was whispering. Steve couldn't make out the words. He strained, his ear expanding, growing larger than his head. He seemed so close this time. If he could only stay asleep long enough. Then he heard it. For the first time the words became clear. Susan was . . . dead!

Fleske took a step toward Barth, his shoes creaking. The noise pulled Steve out of the dream. He opened his eyes, saw the man bearing down on him with the needle. And he remembered everything.

Reaching the third floor, Zavorin raced down the hallway.

Fleske approached the bed. Steve didn't move.

One by one the images of the past months rose in Steve's mind. Andrei, his supposed friend, a KGB agent who'd used him as a courier. Dahlia, always there, who must have been watching him for the Mossad. Abrams, who'd duped him into the trip to Russia. Michael, who interrogated him in London. Fayim, who'd been put on trial. Zev, who was dead. The Colonel, who murdered Susan. And Susan, who had . . .

Fleske pushed the needle into the boy's unresisting arm, readying his finger on the syringe. For a moment their eyes met. Fleske felt the lack of fear, the depth of the loneliness there, and hesitated.

Alexandr Zavorin burst into the room.

In a flash of motion he drew the Baretta from his coat pocket and fired. The silent bullet exploded in Fleske's head. Blood gushed from the wound. He fell forward. Barth watched the red pool forming on the floor.

The rush of faces and memories continued to appear and vanish in his mind. Whenever he tried to hold one it faded, drifting out of reach. Then an image stuck. Susan. He saw her face, listened to her voice—trying to fight the pain. She had been a CIA agent, he her assignment. She'd been no better than the rest of them. She'd lied, used him. The hurt was overwhelming. He squeezed his eyes, trying to will her out of his mind. But some part of him wouldn't let go.

Steve failed to notice Zavorin moving closer, pulling the syringe from his arm. His mind was racing. They'd used him, all of them: the Israelis, the Americans, the British, the Russians. He could hear them, speaking different languages, saying the same thing. Their words poured down his throat like a stream of venom, choking him. He wanted to vomit them back up. But he couldn't.

Zavorin dropped the syringe on the floor. It was over. He had won. In a short while he and Barth would be in a safe-house where the KGB general could . .

Suddenly Steve jumped out of bed and ran across the room. He had made a decision. He would join Robinson . . . Susan . . . Andrei . . . fling himself through the window, end it all. Zavorin, realizing what the boy was about to do, rushed toward him. The door opened. Zavorin spun around. A bullet exploded from the hallway and slammed into his chest.

"Steve. Don't!"

Something familiar in the words reached him, touched some deeply buried feeling. Inches short of the window he stopped. He turned toward the door. His knees buckled. His pulse pounded wildly. It was Susan!

Susan wiped the prints off her pistol and place it in Fleske's inert hand.

"The authorities will assume they killed each other. I've got to get you out of here. There are back stairs where we won't be seen." She put an arm around him and gently held him.

His whole body felt weak. His words broke as he talked. "They told me you were dead."

Tears rolled along his nose, into his moustache, and down through his beard. She took his face in her hands and kissed it, fighting her own tears. "Steve, please believe me, I wasn't briefed about the operation, about anything, until after I left the hotel that afternoon. I intended to return."

He cried freely now. "But what about Moscow, the body in the car?"

"The Israelis substituted the corpse of a girl who'd died the day before. I don't know how, but they found someone the right age. Afterwards I used a forged exit visa to leave the country."

Steve wiped his eyes with the back of his hand and looked at Zavorin lying dead on the floor.

"He's a KGB general," she said softly. "The Israelis leaked a phony story to East German Intelligence, luring him here. The head of the Israeli secret service called me from Vienna this morning. He never wanted you killed. All this was a plot to trap the Russians." Susan looked down, saw the syringe lying next to Zavorin's body and placed it in her purse. She slipped her arm around Steve's waist. "Come on, let's go."

In Jerusalem Yehuda Shamir, head of Operational Planning, waited as the Colonel leafed through the morning's requisition files. As the head of Israeli Intelligence neared the bottom of the pile Shamir shifted position in the overstuffed chair.

"There's one thing that bothers me," he said. "Why did you let Zavorin kill Phillip Fleske?"

The Colonel seemed engrossed in one of the reports. "The CIA wanted to retire him. He refused to resign. They asked us not to intervene." The Mossad chief sipped from the glass of water at his side. Finishing the report, he looked over a cable bill for newspaper items transmitted daily from Moscow, then handed the bill to Shamir.

"Cancel this for me. I'll no longer be needing *Pravda*'s obituary pages."

"Done," Shamir said. "But what about the soccer scores?"

"Soccer scores?" For a moment the Colonel looked puzzled. Then a smile pushed up his face. "Oh, yes, I'd forgotten about those. By all means, cancel them too."